Shadow Work

A Guide to Integrating Your Dark Side for Spiritual Awakening

Your Free Gift
(only available for a limited time)

Thanks for getting this book! If you want to learn more about various spirituality topics, then join Mari Silva's community and get a free guided meditation MP3 for awakening your third eye. This guided meditation mp3 is designed to open and strengthen ones third eye so you can experience a higher state of consciousness. Simply visit the link below the image to get started.

https://spiritualityspot.com/meditation

Table of Contents

Introduction

The trouble with the world today is that we're all suffering from the continued ignorance of our shadow selves. Depression, anxiety, war, and strife result from the collective shadow we all must face, starting with our personal ones. Suppose you've noticed that you've been going through harder times than usual, sabotaging yourself, ruining your prospects, relationships, and more. In that case, it might be that your shadow is asking you to pay attention to it. It's time to integrate your shadow so you can find your true, authentic self and finally heal.

Without integrating the parts of us that we've rejected, there's no chance for us to be able to connect to our souls as we're meant to. We can't find it in ourselves to grow personally, let alone spiritually. The fact that you've decided to read this book says you're aware that you need to heal yourself and look at those parts of yourself that you've rejected for a long time.

Unlike other books on this topic, this one is very easy to read, and the concepts are explained in a way anyone can grasp. Whether you're new to the process of shadow work or have been at this a while, you will find countless nuggets of gold within these pages to mine and make your life richer. Everything is written in simple English, with no esoteric concepts that might confuse the readers.

If you're ready to do the work and redeem all parts of yourself, you're in the perfect spot to do so! Keep an open mind and get ready to become whole again.

Chapter One: Shadow Work 101

What Is the Shadow?

The shadow is a term used in metaphysics to describe the sum totality of our unconscious mind. It can be viewed as an archetype consisting of instinctual elements and emotions, representing the "dark" part of ourselves. Shadows are largely considered taboo because they are negative and uncontrollable. However, shadows are also necessary for our psychological well-being. The shadow is also described as an "other half" that exists with a person. It is considered the part of us that is not of good moral character, but others cannot see it because it is an undiscovered repressed part of ourselves. This leads to a lack of self-acceptance and confidence in one's own personality.

What Is Shadow Work?

Bring your unconscious mind to consciousness.

https://www.pexels.com/photo/adult-anger-art-black-background-356147/

The concept of shadow work refers to the process of bringing our unconscious mind into consciousness. This is done by allowing one's dark side to come out through visualization or dreams, then embracing it and not trying to hide it. With practice, the shadow will be integrated with the "light" side of ourselves and make us whole people.

Shadow work can be used as a tool in psychology and spirituality. It is used in psychology when one wishes to uncover repressed memories and can also be applied in spirituality when seeking greater knowledge of one's soul and its purpose. Among other things, shadow work is known for helping people become more aware of the things that interfere with their daily lives and what they need to do to heal themselves. This is accomplished by coming in contact with your shadow and learning how to embrace it. One seeks to understand their shadow and confront it with the light to heal the inner conflicts within themselves. Many people see the shadow as a negative thing that can only be understood when completely unearthed. However, this isn't completely accurate. After all, the shadow is also made up of some of the good things you've rejected because other people didn't accept them when you were younger.

How Is the Shadow Self Born?

Your shadow (often referred to as the "shadow self") is born when you are young, probably at a very early age. Our environment and the way we were affirmed or rejected by our parents in the first few years of our lives will play an important role in whether or not we develop a healthy sense of self. Even the shiniest of people have their dark side. This is because all humans are born with instincts, which means they will inherently wish to pursue pleasure and avoid pain. Those who cannot accept this side of themselves will develop shame as a result. These individuals usually become perfectionists and are never satisfied with their performance, no matter what.

The shadow is born from the things you reject about yourself and the bad times you experienced as a child. It consists of all the things in life that are unpleasant for us to think about, yet we suppress them and refuse to acknowledge their existence. Doing this causes us to take on destructive characteristics within ourselves to avoid dealing with the pain we have created. These characteristics can be anything from addiction problems, perfectionism, and low self-esteem.

Why You Should Meet Your Shadow

As Carl Jung said, "One does not become enlightened by imagining figures of light, but by making the darkness conscious." It is important to understand that shadows cannot be avoided. They are a part of every human being and are inescapable. Understanding this concept is an important step in learning to love yourself. As a result of your shadow work, you'll be able to acknowledge your bad side without shame and find peace with it. You'll also be able to discover and appreciate the good within you that has been hidden away for years and finally appreciate it as something worthwhile rather than rejecting it.

Jung also said, "Everyone carries a shadow, and the less it is embodied in the individual's conscious life, the blacker and denser it is." The shadow often takes on an animalistic form when we are young due to our experiences. We could be shy, quiet, introverted, or always try to be the center of attention. These characteristics are simply traits that we want others to see - not ones we wish to hide. However, those who repress their shadow prevent themselves from being able to grow into more mature and spiritually aware individuals capable of *bearing* the burdens that come with living in this world instead of being crushed by them.

When we repress the shadow, we do so because we are ashamed of it. When it was born into the world, we were small children and had no idea what a shadow was, what it meant, and why it was there. As a result, we viewed this part of ourselves as something that would cause harm to other people if they were to find out about it. This causes us to hide from our emotions, which causes us to feel isolated from the world. The repression of the shadow also makes us unable to grow to understand who we truly are, and it also makes us more susceptible to projecting our anger onto others.

How Shadow Work Leads to Spiritual Awakening

When you face your shadow, you come face to face with yourself. This is the only way we can ever have self-knowledge and a real awareness of who we are. Usually, people do not like looking at their shadows; so many have psychological problems because they're scared to know what's underneath all that clutter in their minds. It's easier for them to give in to their addictions and let the lies take over their lives and control who they think they are in society.

Shadow work involves a difficult and sometimes painful process of bringing your unconscious into the light of consciousness. It allows you to come to a point where you discover your repressed inner aspects. Your shadow is not something to be feared but rather a part of you that needs to be understood and embraced as your nature. Your conscious mind also needs to know how to work with it for you to reach spiritual awakening. Unfortunately, many people do not understand that their psyche or unconscious mind has a purpose and function and often reject this momentous fact.

How Does Shadow Work, Work?

Shadow work is a long process of conscious discovery during which you confront your repressed personality traits (personalities and behavior patterns) and become the practitioner of the Self. It is this self-knowledge that leads to personal enlightenment and spiritual awakening. During shadow work, one learns to see oneself as part of the inner and outer world. When we can perceive ourselves fully, we transcend the boundaries between inner and outer experience.

In Jungian psychology, shadow work entails the visual mental imagery necessary for dealing with unconscious psychological issues such as aggression. One must learn how to deal with and visualize the shadow rather than allowing it to consume one's life. Many people who undergo shadow work find it difficult and frustrating. Although many of us want to deny our true personality, there is no getting around the fact that *we are who we are.* You don't have to change your shadow - you simply have to accept it for what it is. Once you can do this, your shadow will no longer take control over the direction of your life, and it will cease being a hindrance in your spiritual awakening process.

Carl Jung was aware of the key importance of the shadow. He wrote about the necessity of understanding how one's shadow is necessary for growth and maturity. He even made explicit statements about why one needs to work on their shadow side to be free of its negative influences and destructive behaviors. Jung considered this aspect to be a vital step toward self-knowledge and personal enlightenment. Though we are all marked by our shadow, we can learn to reconcile it with the rest of who we are.

Myths about Shadow Work

Let's address some of the common myths and misconceptions surrounding the concepts of shadow work and the shadow itself.

1. **You're a bad person for having a shadow**: The shadow isn't inherently evil. It is a part of you that was never explored - it only became associated with negative emotions based on external social archetypes.

2. **You're alone in wanting to work on your shadow:** Many people want to work through their shadows and spiritual awakenings. In fact, it's a large community of people who are interested in the same topics and have been struggling with the same issues you have.
3. **You're weak if you don't want to deal with your shadow:** Many people avoid working through their shadows until they feel ready. Waiting doesn't make you weak or a coward; the fact is, none of us knows when we will be ready to deal with our emotional issues. Sometimes we can go through a dark period lasting many years without ever confronting it. When it's time, you'll know it.
4. **Your shadow isn't important:** Your shadow is an integral part of who you are and why you are the way you are today. It needs to be understood if you want to break the bonds of your past and begin a new phase of spiritual awakening. You're wrong if you think you can get rid of it and not have any consequences.
5. **Shadow work is impossible and pointless:** No, it doesn't have to be either. There is nothing to be afraid of, and there are plenty of reasons why shadow work can be worthwhile. It can help you cope with the emotions of your past and give you a better understanding of yourself and your identity. If you've been self-sabotaging yourself and can't figure out why perhaps it's time to say hello to the darkness.

How the Shadow Self Sabotages

Your shadow self can keep you from making money: Your shadow can be a major obstacle behind your lack of financial gain. Since your shadow is a side of yourself that you have repressed and labeled negative, it tends to have a dark and destructive view of money. You may be unable to see anything positive about money because you subconsciously fear it (or were never taught this positive perspective). If you are consistently making sub-par money, it could be because your shadow self is leading you into situations that will make more sense to you to deal with your emotions. It could also be that your true talents, which would bring you success, are buried in the shadow and need to be brought to light to do well.

Your shadow sabotages love relationships: One of the ways in which your shadow can cause problems in love relationships is by undermining what's good about them. It always seeks to keep you from being happy. If you work through your shadow, it will change its ways and let you healthily experience love. Many things can keep your shadow from allowing the good things in your relationship to blossom. Perhaps a part of you desires to remain single and isolated (the loner archetype), or you want something more than what is available (the envious archetype). Perhaps also, you're unable to love because of the fear of rejection (an aspect of yourself that puts up emotional walls when others get too close), which could also be why you attract the wrong partners.

Your shadow can prevent you from having a healthy body: Your shadow self could also be behind your body's lack of health. Perhaps you're unaware of your sensitivity to certain foods or not getting enough sun and exercise. It could also be that your need for control leads you to do too much for yourself instead of doing the things which will make your body happy (like treating it with some delicious food). You might even be unable to lose weight because your shadow aspect feels unsafe and views fat as a protective mechanism.

Your shadow can keep you from enjoying life: Your shadow self could be the problem behind your inability to enjoy life. Perhaps there is too much anxiety and fear in your life - or you are always trying to control everything around you instead of allowing yourself to live spontaneously and enjoy the moment. Working on your shadow can also help increase the happiness in your life. It can show you how to work through your past emotions and let go of them so you can enjoy new experiences. It will also teach you how to accept yourself for who you are and stop getting mad at yourself when things aren't going your way.

Your shadow makes it hard for people to love you: Your shadow can make it difficult for others to see the good things about you. Maybe you're the sort of person who cannot see the good in yourself, talk down on yourself and act out so much that you convince others that you truly aren't worthy of their love. Then they will be more likely to dismiss or abandon you or make your relationships more difficult. You may even attract people who don't care about your needs, and it will take them longer to come around once they've gotten to know you better.

Quiz: How Dominant Is Your Shadow?

1. I believe that something is wrong with me that requires me to constantly control everything around me.
2. I feel like nothing I do is good enough, no matter how much I achieve or what others say about it.
3. My need to be in control of everything around me prevents anyone from getting too close to me and hurts my relationships.
4. I have trouble seeing the good in myself, and I overreact every time someone has a compliment to give.
5. My mood depends on what is going on around me and how things are going. If people start making a fuss, it will be hard for me to remain happy.
6. I feel unhappy with myself even though it doesn't seem that way to everyone.
7. My projects sometimes go bad, and it seems like things are crumbling apart around me, despite my best efforts.
8. Everything around me seems to fall apart because I am too attached, and my emotions are getting in the way of my best efforts.
9. I find myself suddenly and inexplicably overcome with negative emotions.
10. I somehow manage to do or say just the perfect thing to ruin my chances at success.

If you answered yes to six or more of these questions, your shadow is likely dominant and asks that you address it now.

Chapter Two: Discovering and Accepting Your Shadow

Before we talk about what is required for you to discover your shadow (let alone get comfortable enough to accept it), we need to define the keywords "discovery" and "acceptance." The discovery process is about finding something that has always been wherever it is. It's about disclosing the location or whereabouts of whatever you seek. The point to note here is that sometimes you cannot find what you're looking for, and this is why many people do not even know that they have a shadow aspect. In fact, you might be able to think of someone right now who you could never envision having a shadow side. For instance, the thought that Mother Theresa would have a darker aspect is something many cannot fathom.

Acceptance means coming to terms with the existence or truth of something. It's about the process of learning what the thing is and knowing that it is valid as it is, rather than seeking to get rid of or fight it. Upon learning that we all have a shadow, some people seek to abolish it, but that's not how it works. You want to integrate the shadow with the light because it is a part of you. If you reject a part of yourself, you only render yourself more helpless to the shadow. In fact, it is because of rejection that your shadow self came to exist in the first place.

What It Means to Discover and Accept Your Shadow

You might have difficulty believing that you have a shadow side, but think of it this way. Everyone has something dark in them. Maybe you're prone to being unnecessarily mean sometimes or taking pleasure in the misfortune of others. Or, maybe the more insecure part of you wants everyone around you to be exactly as miserable and self-doubting as you so that they validate your feelings with their actions. The point is that everyone has some kind of dark aspect, but it's not necessarily because they are terrible people. It's more about their shadow side being constantly there but kept under wraps until they feel the need to rise and reveal themselves. When your shadow comes out and goes active, you may or may not be in a "bad" mood. You might be in a pessimistic or anxious state, but the person inside - who has repressed it for so long - could be far worse than you realize.

Many people fear their shadow side so much that they go on living as if it isn't even there. This can sometimes be a kind of coping mechanism but also a way of denying your true self or your shadow self. This is why it's essential to discover and accept your shadow. It's the best way to accomplish spiritual well-being and awakening.

What Is Spiritual Awakening, and How Is It Connected to the Shadow Self?

Spiritual awakening is a broad term that refers to the experience you undergo as you move from being unconscious and unaware to more conscious and aware. This includes having control over your life situations, thoughts, and emotions. It's about awakening to the meaning of life. To get a clearer idea of what this means, let's analyze that thought process through the lens of Carl Jung.

Carl Jung believed that to become more conscious and aware, we must confront our shadow parts and make peace with them. To do this, we must release the repressed and twisted inside us. We must let go of the pain and suffering that a misguided identity or ego can cause. We must also accept ourselves and realize that we are all human beings who make mistakes. At the same time, we must recognize our potential for greatness and do what it takes to get there.

All of this is connected to a concept called individuation. It basically refers to your identity or ego becoming individualized, so you are no longer like everyone else but instead shaped by your perspective & experiences in life thus far. Individuation is one of the most important concepts in psychology, especially because it applies so strongly to your shadow self. Embracing your unconscious thinking and emotions and learning to work with them for good leads to individuation, which allows you to awaken spiritually.

Why You Must Accept Your Flaws to Progress Spiritually

Accepting your flaws takes away the power they have over you: One of the ways you can start waking up to your shadow self is by accepting it. This means you stop struggling against it or try hiding it from others. Instead, you realize that the shadow self is okay and part of who you are. Admitting that we have these flawed perspectives and beliefs can be very dark and painful at times, but as long as we don't reject them, they won't control us and make us sick or unhappy.

Accepting your flaws will help you grow: Another way accepting your flaws helps you is by making you more aware of things. If you're constantly fighting and escaping your shadow self, it's hard to be aware and see that things in this world can help shape who you become. However, accepting everything about who you are and what makes up your personality gives you a greater perspective. Plus, we all have our share of flaws. Rather than being ashamed of these human characteristics, embrace them and do something about them.

Accepting your flaws will allow you to become more like yourself: When you accept your flaws, you start realizing that you're not who you thought you were. For example, say that someone believed they were a kind and loving person, but then they discover their dark side that wants to hurt people. This can be very confusing and scary for them because they were raised to believe that bad things will happen to them if they behave badly. However, suppose they stop fighting against themselves and learn to accept who they are inside and what their shadow self has taught them throughout their lives. In that case, it's easier to see the truth about themselves. When one confronts the truth about themselves, they can effectively work to improve.

Accepting both the light and dark sides of yourself will help you be more objective: By accepting everything about who we are and what shapes our personalities, we stop projecting our flaws onto other people. For example, if you struggle with negative thoughts, you may project these thoughts onto the people around you. Instead of taking responsibility for them, it's easier to blame them. This very common pattern leads to fighting, arguments, and strife that can destroy relationships.

Signs of Discovering and Accepting the Shadow

Let's look at six signs that indicate you're on track to finding and accepting your shadow.

1. **What other people do no longer triggers you like it used to:** When you start accepting your shadow self, it almost feels like the world has become safer and more *right.* That's because, now that you've accepted who you are, what other people do is no longer a trigger for you. This means that being upset with people for doing something is just a misunderstanding and not about who these people are to you.
2. **You no longer engage in denial or blaming others:** This is a key sign you're getting close to discovering and accepting your shadow. You no longer deny who you are or what these negative thoughts tell you. You realize that there's nothing wrong with yourself and your subconscious; those thoughts are just a projection of how you feel deep down inside. You stop blaming others for your struggles and no longer blame yourself.

3. **You no longer get upset or angry when you see others with dark sides:** You realize that all human beings have good and bad sides. These character traits may come out at different times in a person's life; who they are today results from their earlier experiences, and you know that they were raised by flawed parents or in a less-than-perfect environment.
4. **You're no longer afraid to be seen or heard:** Once you've accepted your shadow self, you gain the courage to come out of hiding. This means that you no longer fear the light because you realize *it can't hurt you.* After all, the light and dark parts of yourself make up who you are and what makes up your personality. This is another big step in healing because it allows you to do what feels comfortable without living a lie anymore.
5. **You no longer feel alone or isolated:** It's common for people with a shadow self to feel disconnected from others because they have trouble accepting their flaws and being seen in public. However, once they accept them, they see that there's nothing wrong with them and start enjoying the company of others again.

Side Effects of Shadow Work

You start to notice how you've deceived yourself.

When doing shadow work, you will likely suddenly notice how your mind has distorted the way you perceive the world around you - and how you perceive yourself. You'll find that some of your perceptions couldn't be further from the truth. You will also be easier on people who haven't gotten to the point of being able to see their self-deceit either.

Tip: At first, it can be rather problematic when you discover how much you've been blind to, but the key to working through that confusion is to be gentle with yourself. Don't allow yourself to wallow in self-hate or self-pity.

You realize just how much you've struggled to control things – and that you no longer need to do that.

You may have done your best to rein yourself in because you don't want to act out or may have tried to control others around you to create your "ideal" version of how life should be. When you're doing shadow work, you'll start to realize the futility of trying to make everything perfect. You will naturally relinquish your need to be in charge of everything all the time, which can be incredibly freeing.

Tip: In the beginning, it's going to be pretty scary. This is because you've gone your entire life making sure there are no unknowns and that you're always ready even for the most unlikely events and scenarios. Learn to think of this as a rollercoaster. You're on the ride; you can't get off until it's over, so you might as well turn those screams of terror into excitement and roll with the process.

You develop a form of tunnel vision when it comes to your creativity.

Accepting your shadow means that you'll be able to easily connect with your creative side, to the exclusion of everything else and without getting distracted. You'll be able to marry different concepts together in a way that works for one and all. The trouble is that some people don't know how to ground their creativity in realism because it's all-new for them, which could lead them to make detrimental decisions, especially in their relationships.

Tip: Enjoy your newfound creativity, but always take a moment to absorb what's really happening in the world around you so that you don't miss the important things and get lost in a never-ending stream of ideas.

You might seem a little cold and standoffish to other people.

As you get more involved in shadow work, you'll find that you're more aware of what others choose to do and say, and you can see through all that right to the heart of their motives. Your ability to see through the heart of a "despicable" person like a serial killer, for instance, will lead to you having a different take on things than most people. In other words, it's not that you'd justify their behavior, but you might be able to see how past trauma and wounds could have led them to become who they were. People might misrepresent your idea as defending evil, but you're not. You're simply more aware of their motivations and more compassionate than others.

Tip: Always strive for mutual understanding in your communications with others, and you shouldn't have a problem connecting with those who matter. Also, it will be clear to those who get it that you're anything but standoffish.

You no longer care for customary ways of doing things.

The thing about our culture and what we hold dear in society is that society itself also has its own shadows. When society deems a thing good or bad, you can rest assured that while people try to be good, their shadows will have the "bad" in them. Those aware of their shadows no longer allow themselves to feel shame about their "wrong" behaviors, choosing to forgive themselves. They know that these desires are in us all, and so they don't care whether or not the world and its traditions deem them to be a terrible person. For instance, maybe in the past, you were a Christian who truly believed it was bad to be rich, but you've now realized that while your desire to be rich would be frowned upon by some Christians, you no longer care for those restrictions; they no longer define you. You can live your life as your authentic self.

Tip: Try to be patient with others. Not everyone is aware of the unnecessary restrictions inherent in tradition and culture, and some people need those structures to have some sense of purpose and stability in their lives. Don't judge them for it.

Things You Can Do to Discover Your Shadow

1. **Look inwards:** Find a quiet place where you can sit alone and listen to what your subconscious says. If you're scared or nervous, acknowledge those feelings and then continue listening to what your inner self says.
2. **Face the things that scare you:** Whatever the monster in the closet is for you, decide that you'll stop running and start facing your fears. By doing this repeatedly, you

realize there's nothing to be afraid of because everything inside of you is normal and okay.

3. **Accept yourself:** Decide that it's okay to accept who you are even if - sometimes -you don't like some things about yourself.
4. **Stop fighting against yourself:** Once you've accepted who you are, stop fighting against your shadow side. In other words, give up the battle that you're not going to be negative anymore. Instead, start looking at negative feelings as a normal part of who you are and what makes up your personality.

Quiz: Have You Truly Discovered and Accepted Your Shadow?

1. Have you accepted who your true self is?
2. Can you accept the negative aspects of your personality by looking at them as a normal part of who you are and what makes up "you"?
3. Do you accept who others are - even if what they *do* bothers or hurts you?
4. Do you find it easier to process your negative emotions and not judge others?
5. Have you stopped blaming others for anxiety, anger, fear, sadness, trouble with social situations, etc.?

If you answered yes to three out of five questions, it means you're making progress with your shadow work; keep working at it!

Chapter Three: The Shadow's Mirror Effect

Mirrors are very important when it comes to spirituality, discovering who you are, and exactly *what it is* you need to heal. Regarding cognitive psychology, many studies have centered on working with mirrors to come to terms with self-consciousness and self-identity. Also, you don't need to think about the mirror effect in terms of working with an actual mirror alone and seeing what the world mirrors back to you. Your experience of the world is just a reflection of who you are. This is a tough bit of truth to chew on, but when you really consider it, you'll see why it's important to change yourself first if you want the world around you to change.

Let's give a little more thought to the concept of mirroring. The mirror will copy what you're observing perfectly and right away. Also, it doesn't have any actual imperfections in how it reflects back to you. They will copy your expressions and can affect you emotionally on an unconscious level. For instance, watching yourself smile in the mirror will naturally induce feelings of happiness within you.

Mirror Work

The mirror effect allows you to see the truth of your soul.
https://www.pexels.com/photo/photo-of-man-looking-at-the-mirror-1134184/

Mirror work is a simple thing that will change your life and help you integrate all aspects of your shadow, including your wounds. This will help you learn to truly love yourself. Rooted in the philosophies of Carl Jung, the mirror work technique was created by Louise Hay to help people learn to love themselves. It's supposed to help you change how you relate with yourself to effectively change how you relate with others and your world. It's meant to teach you to love and care for yourself fully.

If you stare in the mirror for just five minutes, maintaining eye contact with yourself and being gentle about it, you might notice some interesting emotions welling up within you. You may start to feel awkward or a bit embarrassed, and you may even begin to judge and loathe yourself. The question is, why does this happen?

According to Louise Hay, the mirror will always show you what you feel about yourself. It lets you know what holds you back from full self-love and where you're doing just fine. It can also reveal to you the thoughts you've to get rid of or implement to feel more fulfilled. Andy Fox said, "In our own mirror, we can see the soul's truth." You can't hide from the truth, and you'll gain a level of intimacy with it that may leave you feeling uneasy if you don't learn how to silence your inner critic. Things you didn't even know you thought about yourself come to the surface of the conscious mind.

The Pros of Mirror Work with Shadow Work

To be clear, both of these things can be very uncomfortable at first, but when you stick with the process, you'll find incredible healing. These are some of the most powerful processes of ascending spiritually. You won't have to spend money to make this happen or sequester yourself away from life. Mirror work is something you can easily incorporate into your daily life. You only need a mirror, an open mind, and the ability to remain present all through the process. Here's why you should consider doing mirror work:

It's a form of self-love: You'll learn to truly love yourself through mirror work. This is a process that will help you to reflect on your inner light and embrace it fully. It can be quite hard to feel this way when your self-image has been wounded, but you will have no problem healing yourself with such a simple process. You'll learn how to love the person staring back at you in the mirror by accepting yourself for everything that makes up who you are. This isn't easy to do, as your wounds from the past can make it difficult for you to accept and love yourself.

You're forced to face the parts of you that you're not proud of: You'll learn to face and love the parts of your past that you're not proud of and come to grips with who you are and what it is about yourself that makes you who you are today. You'll admit to your mistakes, even those that spurn regrets and make you feel horrible. It's all part of the healing process. You can also actively choose to forgive yourself through this process because forgiveness is a part of healing.

You learn how to be vulnerable: You'll learn how to accept your vulnerabilities and embrace them as a natural part of being alive and a way to help protect yourself from further harm. You can't change your past and the fact that you've made mistakes.

You'll need to work through it to learn how to accept yourself.

You learn to stop judging: One of the most powerful parts of mirror work is that you'll learn how to let go of all the judgments and criticisms you have about yourself. This will help open up your mind and heart so that they're more receptive to healing and more open when it comes to loving yourself and others. When your mind is free from these judgments, you won't feel trapped in a prison of negativity and pain. Instead, you will feel like an open book, ready to receive all the healing you need.

You learn to accept others: When your mind is free from judgments, you can truly make the shift from seeing others as a reflection of your own shadow and how they're hurting or bothering you to seeing them for who they are and the way they feel about themselves. You'll begin to accept others for their gifts and learn to love them on their own terms. Rather than being so caught up in how you think things should be or what other people should be doing, it prevents you from loving yourself and caring about what's going on in your life.

Guide to Mirror Work

1. **Commit to this:** When it comes to mirror work, you have to first decide you're going to see it through. It's a good idea to dedicate about two to five minutes each day at the very least. Ideally, it's best to go for ten minutes per session.
2. **Consider the best time of day to do this work:** You're not going to get better results picking one time of day over another. Most people get into mirror work either first thing when they wake up or the last thing before going to bed. If you like, you can just do it each time you pass by a mirror. If you don't have access to a mirror, you can use your phone camera's selfie option. You're also going to need some privacy, so keep that in mind.
3. **Pick your affirmations:** You can create your own affirmations if you like and work with them because you'll need them to counteract the negative thoughts that will arise as you gently gaze into your eyes in the mirror.

These words will help you reprogram your mind to think better of yourself. You could work with many already scripted affirmations, but in my experience, it's much better to spontaneously allow them to flow in response to whatever you're feeling. For instance, if you notice a feeling of discomfort while sitting in front of the mirror, you can affirm to yourself, "I have a lovely heart and soul," or "I am comfortable with myself, and I accept myself the way I am." At the end of this guide, you will find affirmations you can work with to help you.

4. **Say your affirmation repeatedly, feeling each word:** You should say each affirmation you've chosen to work with at least ten times. You can say them in your mind or out loud. Don't go for 100 repetitions like others recommend because you don't want to turn this into a boring chore and get to the point where the words lose meaning and feeling. Make sure to really ponder what each word means to you, as this is what will create the change you seek. Make sure you're staring yourself right in the eyes as you affirm the words. You can also address yourself using your name, which will drive the message deeper and faster into your unconscious mind.
5. **Welcome the emotions that come up:** As you do this work, you'll feel all sorts of things. Whatever it is that comes up, allow yourself to feel it. It's okay to laugh, cry, or react in any way that feels natural to you. It's good practice to hug yourself as well. It may sound silly, but you're really going to feel it. Some of the things you feel will come from your childhood can be really intense. If that happens, you need to be ready to accept your inner, wounded child as they are. Use reassuring words with them. Let them know you're here for them, love them, and understand them.
6. **Feel your heart:** Keep your hand over it as you do the work. You may feel drawn to rub that area in a circle or pat it gently or firmly. Just give in to the moment and whatever it is you need. If you feel you're too overwhelmed from doing that, it's okay to take a break

and return to the process later. However, the odds are that whatever comes up at the moment is *exactly* what you need to feel and is just right; don't let your emotions and thoughts frighten you. The hand over your heart will help you connect with your body and your true self and put you in touch with the vibration of love.

7. **Write down what you discover**: You'll need a journal to refer to as you do your mirror work. This is because you're going to get insight into your shadow self as you do the work and learn what you need to do and change to bring your shadow self into the rest of you so that you're a fully integrated person. When you write down your insights, you'll have something to reflect on to show you how to live a more fulfilled life. Your journal doesn't need to be organized, and you don't have to write a full book on each session. Just note what you feel and think and the sensations that arose during your session. You don't have to make an entry in your journal every day after the session, but it's worth having one for when you get new, profound insights into your life. It's handy for seeing just how far you've come.

Spot Your Shadow in Action

The thing about the shadow is that it's *not so easy to spot.* It's the part of you that can be really elusive unless - or until - it sabotages your life enough that you have no choice but to pause and ask yourself why nothing works out, despite your best intentions. Here are a few things you can do to catch your shadow in action.

1. **Notice when you make judgments about people.** When you judge others, believe it or not, you're really judging yourself. The reason is that the things that trigger you about other people are the same things that you can consciously or subconsciously recognize in yourself. Your judgments are actually rooted in the weaknesses you perceive. This weakness is what you were taught as a young one and throughout your adult life to suppress and reject, causing it to become part of your shadow. Another

thing to note about judgment is that we only ever judge those who we feel we're better than, those we think we can "lord it over." Yet the funny thing is that the judgments we make say more about us and what makes us insecure than the object of our disdain.

2. **Notice when you project your problems onto other people.** Shadow projection is very real. We get involved in a process to defend ourselves from dealing with our issues. Instead of owning them, part of the rejection process is us casting all the emotions and thoughts we have about ourselves that we don't want to deal with onto someone else. When you don't like a certain thing about yourself, you tend to see it in others whether or not it's there. The more you project your issues onto others, the more you feed your shadow. For instance, you could think of someone as too full of themselves when you're actually an arrogant person. How else would you be able to recognize that attribute in them, real or perceived? This is why those who cheat on their partners or lie to them will accuse their loved ones of doing the same thing. People who don't like their bodies laugh at others for how they look.
3. **Pay attention to your triggers.** When something causes you to have an intense emotional reaction, you should stop and ask yourself why. In being introspective like this, you'll likely see that your shadow is poking its head into the window of your life to say hello. Triggers are often what we have as a result of some event that was traumatic to us that we may have "forgotten" through repression. They're basically your Achilles' heel. When you can take the time to understand your triggers, you'll learn more about your shadow.
4. **Notice your tendency to hurt people when you feel there are no consequences.** For instance, let's assume you engage in trolling others to hurt them online. You're fully aware it's not the right thing to do, yet you do it anyway. Why is that? Your shadow makes itself known in times when there's no consequence to face for your actions and

words. You're unafraid to show the very worst aspects of yourself because, as far as you're concerned, "No one would ever know." So, notice how you deal with things when there's no one around. Even if you're the one person who likes to help the old lady with the grocery bag across the street, pause to ask yourself if this is something you would do if no one were around to notice how nice you are.

5. **Notice how you treat those you're in charge of.** For instance, you could have a terrible time at home, or your boss may have torn you a new one for something. Maybe you perceive in both situations that there's nothing you could do to your lover or your boss, so instead, you take out your frustrations on those who you have authority over. For instance, you could have angry outbursts that aren't justified on those you manage – including your kids. You could even be on the lookout for that one stranger who'll cross your path so that you can let them have it instead.
6. **Pay attention to your penchant for playing the victim card.** If you consider yourself the victim, you always have that "woe is me" attitude going on, wallowing in self-pity. When things go wrong, rather than looking for your part in the problem or considering how to move forward, you'd blame other people. Responsibility is just not your thing. Also, you likely have trouble trusting people because people are the issue as far as you're concerned. You come off as helpless and weak, even though, in an insidious way, that's a method of control as you make others do your bidding out of false obligation and guilt. You have no limits, which in addition to your low confidence, makes you very susceptible to being taken advantage of by the people in your life. You have a "me against the world" attitude, and you're always spoiling for a fight. Those who continue to play victim tend to be miserable because of it, which fuels issues like depression and anxiety. If this sounds like you, know that victimhood is one of the ways the shadow presents itself.

Chapter Four: The Shadow and Authenticity

Authenticity is about being who you really are. We live in a world where daring to be yourself is considered enough to "cancel" you and deem you unfit to be part of a group. In part, we can thank social media - where everyone wants to be relevant and follow the crowd irrespective of one's own perspective. People who have different opinions are being silenced by bullying. Those who don't have enough courage to maintain their difference of opinion feel the pressure to go along with the mob because they've seen what happens when you start singing a slightly different tune.

As a result, it's hard to find authentic people in this day and age. Instead, many of us suppress our truths and the aspects of us that we feel our tribe will not agree with. This, of course, causes the shadow self to grow stronger each day. In the real sense, authenticity is being who you are, regardless of whether anyone is on your side or not. It's daring to be yourself, present your truths as you see them, and remain un-swayed by the threats of being excommunicated from some group or "canceled" on the internet. This, of course, is not an easy thing to do. It can be a constant struggle to not feel the need to curate the best parts of myself from one situation to the next; we struggle with this daily - some more consciously than others.

Inauthenticity, the Shadow, and Spiritual Growth

When you're not true to who you are, you're repressing the aspects that you consider undesirable, which will naturally cause your shadow to grow stronger. It is virtually impossible to grow personally and spiritually if we do not stay true to ourselves. As Carl Jung puts it, "That which you most need will be found where you least want to look." If you've felt like you're stuck in a rut lately, it might be good to consider looking at how authentic you've been lately.

To grow spiritually, you're going to have to live authentically. This means following the urges that your soul lays within your heart. But each time you seek to pursue it only to allow yourself to be silenced for whatever reason, you keep yourself from spiritual growth and expansion.

You must develop the courage to face yourself, your shadow, and your inauthentic behavior. The longer you put it off, the more damage you'll do to yourself, your relationships, and your life. On this inner journey of self-discovery and authenticity, many people experience the depths of despair, which is natural. It's crucial to remember that you need this darkness to see the light.

Becoming conscious of our compulsive patterns (and shedding light on those unconscious ones) will help unify both parts of our psyches. There are many ways to interpret this spiritual growth process in practice, but one thing's for sure: it requires a willingness to face your shadow. Anything less than that will lead to stagnation and isolation.

We need the opportunity to grow to come closer to knowing ourselves, which is why it is important to see our wrongdoings and learn from them. In some cases, that's all we need to release ourselves from a self-loathing perspective. We must become aware of our unconscious, embrace it at times, and know that it is an essential part of who we are.

When you feel stuck, try bringing the shadow into your consciousness by simply observing yourself from a space outside yourself. Try not to attach judgment or criticism to any aspect of yourself (or others), but instead understand that this feeling is rooted within you and is part of how you deal with things. There's no need to blame any person or the circumstances; just observe whatever thoughts come up and keep holding still.

Repression Breeds Regression

One of the best ways to identify something that you're repressing is to look for patterns and behaviors that you create in your life by holding back from these parts of yourself. It's important to understand that the more we repress, the easier it is for us to do so. This, in turn, makes us more susceptible to wild conspiracy theories, where we label people as "bad" and fixate on them obsessively. It's often easy to understand why people feel this way if they have a negative history with certain aspects of their personality.

How can you find peace within if you're repressing a part of yourself? You'll only take many steps backward, spiritually speaking. When fear and judgment exist, we also repress the truth about ourselves because fear keeps us locked in a cycle of continuous suppression of our shadow. When we stop running and hiding from these parts of ourselves and embrace them instead, it goes a long way toward confronting the fears that arise in our lives. This can have great benefits for those who are open to it.

The shadow is not just something that affects or influences us internally; it also affects our external *reality.* You see this in certain political situations where people take on the characteristics of the very person they chose to vilify.

When we repress our shadow, we give it power over us, letting it know we won't fight back and that we'll allow ourselves to be ruled by some part or aspects of ourselves. Or, in some cases, people will hold a grudge against another person and let their mood or emotional state control them because they want to get back at them for one reason or another.

Confronting your shadow is one of the biggest challenges you'll ever face; you'll need the courage to do that. Accept that the shadow lurks within the recesses of the unconscious and that it is largely made up of repressed instinctual drives.

Put Up Your Dukes and Fight for What You Want

When we don't stay true to ourselves, it's easy to get caught up in a cycle of self-loathing where we feel trapped in our bodies and minds. We will often judge ourselves harshly while also judging others. The first step is always to observe yourself without attaching any judgment or criticism to what you find - simply observe it without judgment.

We need to observe these patterns and behaviors in our lives and how they affect us. Let yourself get as much information as you can about these "dark" parts of yourself, then let them go with love. This is how you become authentic and allow yourself to awaken spiritually.

Some people learn to ignore or mask the shadow, while others act it out negatively. You'll find that some people are more affected by their shadow than others, but all of us are affected by our selfishness at times. It's normal - it's just part of being human - but not something we have to let rule over us.

To awaken from this shadow self and become authentic, we must shed light on our unconscious, compulsive behavior. The more we struggle, the stronger it will hold onto us. The more we let go of it, the less of an effect it will have on us. You'll learn to accept that you have a shadow part of yourself - just like everyone else.

A Guide to Identifying Your Authentic Self

Identifying your authentic self is a very personal process and requires a willingness to explore yourself. It's not about being perfect; it's about being real with yourself and learning to accept that part of yourself that you don't really like.

When you're young, you often don't have the necessary tools to uncover your shadow or get to know your authentic self. This is why staying connected with your inner child as much as possible is important. Your child is always waiting for you as it understands that nobody loves them unconditionally as they do. They crave acceptance and understanding from their caregivers, even when they don't necessarily deserve it.

It's important to be patient with yourself as you go through this process. The more you are willing to take the time to self-reflect, the greater chances you have of uncovering some things that will make you a happier person.

There are a few things that will help in identifying your authentic self:

1. **Begin taking personal inventory:** First, check in with yourself to know when you feel most honest and authentic. You'll have to be courageous as you ask yourself questions and tell yourself the truth. Truth is important because the last thing you want is more repression by hiding behind a mask or embodying values that aren't true to who you are. When you're clear on what matters to you, it will be easier to take action and make decisions. So, ask yourself, where do you feel most alive? Who do you love to hang out with the most; who brings out the best in you? What sorts of activities do you love to engage in? What aspects of your life are you most unhappy or upset about? What is it that you *know is* toxic and needs to go?

   From there, you can go even deeper with this. For instance, whenever you're in a situation that doesn't feel good to you, take a second to figure out what's going on. Who's with you when you feel less than good? What are the emotions coursing through you, and what is the price you have to pay when these negative situations happen? Do the same for situations where you feel your best and most authentic self. This will help you see what you've got to change.

2. **Ground yourself in the present moment**: Figure out what's happening in the *here and now.* The less attention you pay to the past, the more room there is to make proper decisions in the future. The more you relax and go with the flow, the easier it will be to act authentically.

To do this well, you shouldn't be focused on thinking about things that have already happened. When something triggers an emotion or a feeling inside you, let it be there until it dies down on its own. Then take a few minutes, or as long as it takes, to figure out how you feel about what's happening at this moment and how your past experiences affected your current feelings.

3. **Create a support system you can lean on:** One of the most important things you can do is create relationships that ground you and support you in being your authentic self. Surround yourself with people who are committed to your success and help you move forward positively. Find people who will understand your struggles, doubts, and fears; they can help when things get difficult. As long as they're also committed to personal growth, they'll have enough integrity that they won't exploit your weaknesses – or your ability to be vulnerable. Having a strong support system is one of the most important parts of personal transformation because it helps minimize the stress from within so you can focus on what's happening in the present moment.
4. **Always speak the truth with love and assertion:** Don't be afraid to speak up for yourself. You want to express what you truly want and how you truly feel about something. It will likely be a challenge and can even result in unhappiness if you don't do so from a place of love and care for yourself. As long as it's coming from your heart, other people will always respect this truth that hasn't been watered down by compromise or a lack of assertiveness.
5. **Don't dwell on what others think**: Another way to ensure that your authentic self comes through is never taking things personally when others act negatively toward you or criticize your actions or choices. What matters is how they treat those who they love and care about. When you see the world through this lens, you see that people's actions are always determined by how they feel about themselves and their perceptions of others. These are *their issues,* not yours. This doesn't mean you need to

tolerate abusive behavior from others, but you can avoid pain if you focus on yourself and how other people treat important people in their lives.

6. **Try being authentic with another person**: Experiment with being your authentic self with another person or even several people. You'll most likely be surprised about how well this works out as long as you're willing to take a risk and put yourself out there. It will sometimes be uncomfortable, but it will be a great learning experience as you get accustomed to being authentic with other people. Be completely honest about your desires and needs, even when it might make you feel vulnerable. The only way you can get what you want is to let the chips fall where they may so that you'll learn from your mistakes and mistakes from others in return. It's important to take responsibility for what happens rather than blaming the person you love or the situation that's causing you stress or sadness in your life.
7. **Feel your emotions as they are**: Emotions aren't bad, and you don't have to deny them or keep them bottled up inside of you. Learn to understand the signs that your authentic self is trying to communicate to you through these emotions. As your awareness increases and the more in touch you are with the present moment and what's going on inside of yourself, you can be certain about what is real and what isn't. This will help you make better decisions as your authentic self takes over and guides the way forward so that you're living a life that feels good, honest, authentic, and true.

Chapter Five: The Shadow and Relationships

The shadow can affect your relationships.

https://www.pexels.com/photo/photo-of-people-doing-fist-bump-3184430/

What are relationships? These are the connections that exist between two different people or parties. For the most part, when people talk about relationships, they're talking about romantic connections, but it's basically the way we relate with ourselves and those around us. So, technically, it's about romantic partnerships, family, friends, and coworkers. Relationships are about connection, usually rooted in emotion. You have a relationship with the world around you as long as you exist. Whether that relationship is warm or cold is a different matter entirely.

The impact of your shadow self can affect all areas of your life, including your relationships. How you relate with others and feel about yourself is in correlation with your shadow. It's not that other people are causing you to feel a certain way about yourself; you are unknowingly projecting negative characteristics onto people to protect yourself.

The Shadow in Marriage

A funny thing about marriage is that the things that draw a couple together in the first place are the same things that often turn out to be problematic later on. What was once attractive becomes rather repulsive. For instance, let's say a man was drawn to a woman's warmth and her ability to connect with people emotionally. Later on, he may think of her warmth and desire for connection as her being annoying and too much in his business. He may think of it as her being shallow and ingenuine in her affection.

When it comes to the woman, she may once have loved him because he was a dependable person whose reactions she could easily predict, who made her feel secure with him. Later on, she may come to look at those same qualities as him being quite the bore. She may consider his predictability as being set in his ways and stifling. So, it turns out that the things she once admired in him are the very things she loathes. The same qualities they both loved about each other are now relabeled and hated. What changed? Nothing - on the surface of things. However, both of them began to let their shadows take the reins and distort reality; this may be a cry for attention to the darkness that needs embracing in each person - and in the relationship itself.

How the Shadow Affects Your Relationships

If you're growing in love and intimacy with those who matter to you, it is important to get in touch with your shadow self. Shadow behavior causes you to relinquish responsibility for your part and blame other people for your situation and circumstances. When you're exhibiting shadow behavior, you're basically acting out based on the needs of your inner child, which were long ignored. It's what makes you want to isolate yourself and feel rage and depression. Often, those who haven't addressed their hidden anger and anxiety that bubbles beneath the surface will have to deal with their shadow self or face the consequences that do not positively affect the relationships in their lives.

Your shadow self can cause issues with your relationship by making you feel like you need to protect yourself from those you love whenever it's triggered. This is why you get into arguments that don't make sense or are difficult to resolve. Repression of your shadow's undesired aspects can lead you to act in ways that aren't true to who you really are. You've got a mask over your soul, which is not good for creating authentic relationships based on love and truth. When we're being inauthentic, the impulse is to run away from those who are healthy and have nothing but love for us because we think the worst parts of us are undeserving of their love.

For instance, if you're always hiding the bits of you that you're ashamed of, you'll find it impossible to relax. You'll always be on the lookout for something that might expose you and make you feel vulnerable; therefore, you avoid and run away before it gets close to you. When people want to get close, you prevent all forms of intimacy. You may not even know what blocks you have that make you continue acting the way you do. That's your shadow work. That's why you find it so hard to maintain relationships and why you keep running from others who want something deep with you, whether that's as friends, family, or romantic partners.

Locked within the shadow are the emotions of guilt and shame. You have to keep in mind that you are dealing with not one shadow *but two* when it comes to relationships. If both partners in a relationship, friendship, or family connection are unaware of the shadow self, it can be destructive and problematic. No matter the relationship in question, it is important for all parties to do the work of discovering their shadows and working with them. If you are single and are thinking about getting into a relationship, it would be best to sit down and work through your shadow issues before you connect with someone else. Otherwise, the chances that things will go from loving to toxic are quite high.

The Key to Healing Relationships

Choosing to understand your shadow is the first important step towards developing better relationships all around. What does it mean to know the traits you've hidden away from yourself? It's about observing your reactions and noticing when they come not from a place of love but from a darker place. It's also a good idea to notice when your partner acts out from their own shadow. When you become familiar with your shadow, you will notice that you no longer react without thinking, and your actions are rooted in compassion. You will notice that you and your partner are human beings deserving of respect and love and aren't simply meant to be used for each other's selfish ends.

To put this another way, getting friendly with your shadow will let you take part in your relationship in a healthy way. You simply must come to terms with the emotions, impulses, and needs that you've hidden. When you do, you'll be able to understand them with ease and notice when they arise. You'll also be able to communicate that to your partner, who, if they've got any understanding about shadow selves, will be able to help you. You'll realize that when it comes to dealing with shadows, it's a collaborative effort that requires being open and honest. There's no room for pointless ugly arguments.

Being in a relationship with someone can be a good thing because you can both act as a mirror for each other. The important thing is that you are both conscious of the importance of looking at your shadow aspects. You can use what you learn from your reflection as a tool to help you heal the parts that are still wounded.

Doing shadow work in your relationship is incredibly wholesome because it makes you compassionate towards each other. All that is required is for both partners to be willing and able to dig deep into their pasts and take a critical look at what they deeply fear. The more willing you are to face your shadows, the better your relationship will become because you can recognize other people's shadows and tolerate them far better than you used to. Don't waste another minute of your time blaming the other person for the fears you have not yet worked through and a past they can do nothing to change. Instead, bless them for the opportunity they have given you because they act as a mirror. This is how to develop healthy and long-lasting relationships.

A Guide to Working with the Shadow for Better Relationships

1. **Realize the difference between the shadow and the ego:** The shadow is what makes you who you are. It's also what makes you human as opposed to a robotic machine. The ego is all about being in your power and acting in a self-consistent, controlling, and self-serving manner. As long as the ego isn't falling apart on the inside, it can be controlled, repressed, or can be hidden away from the world. But if your shadow begins to influence your behavior and decisions, it's time to take care of this part for yourself and others around you to begin to live an authentic life.
2. **Take care of yourself from the inside out:** As you begin to get in touch with the shadow side, you need to take care of yourself. This is about your emotional and spiritual health as much as anything else. You can't continue to just push things away or make excuses for what you, someone else, or a situation have done. Taking responsibility for everything, including your shadow side and your strengths and weaknesses, allows you to face what's going on inside of you and be honest about where you are today.

3. **Realize that no one is perfect:** The path of personal growth involves making mistakes and learning from them so that it's not a continual process. The shadow is the part of you that you aren't aware of when it comes to what you want and need or how you feel about others, situations, or even your behavior. Other people might also have a shadow, so they're not always as honest and open as you think they should be. This is why working with the shadow can benefit all of your relationships to some degree. Cut your partner some slack because they're not perfect either. Encourage them as they also work through their shadow issues.
4. **Accept the fact that life isn't fair:** The reality is that life isn't fair. People you have close relationships with will make mistakes, take advantage of others, and let their egos get in the way when convenient for them. To have a healthy relationship with others, you need to accept this reality. How they respond and act negatively is often more an indication of their issues than it is of you. So, when it comes to letting go of your expectations, don't blame them or feel victimized by them but begin to focus on yourself and what you can learn from them in the present moment.
5. **Let go of trying to control others:** You ultimately can't control the behavior of others. Therefore, it's best to focus on your behavior and how you can change it rather than trying to get others to change. The more you try to control someone else, the more they will act out, and the worse it will get between the two of you. It's better to let go of trying to control others and focus on changing yourself because this gives you something constructive to do instead of blaming them for what they do or don't do.
6. **Get in touch with your anger:** Sometimes, when people have a shadow side, pent-up anger has built up inside them due to their circumstances growing up. This is even truer if they've been abused in some way. This can also happen if you've had your guilt and shame issues as a child. Getting in touch with your anger is about learning

where this emotion stems from to embrace it, understand it, and use it to help you become more of who you are.

7. **Practice forgiveness:** When the anger builds up, try forgiving those who have hurt or betrayed your relationship. You might need to take this step before you forgive yourself and others for what happened because the process of forgiving someone else takes a great amount of work and is often uncomfortable times. Once you forgive, it'll give you a sense of freedom and will let you feel your authentic self more freely.
8. **Establish boundaries:** Setting boundaries is a way of maintaining and holding onto your integrity and being honest about what you need or don't need in your life. This also helps to let others know that this is part of who you are, so they understand you're not going to get manipulated or used. Suppose you don't establish boundaries early on with others. In that case, people will continue to take advantage of their power over you until it eventually becomes too much for either of you to handle.
9. **Accept that you're not perfect:** The biggest mistake that many people make when working on their personal growth is that they become too attached to perfection. If they don't achieve it or fall short of this, they feel like a failure, which is an unrealistic expectation to have. You need to be realistic about what you can and can't do and accept this as part of who you are so that you're not always trying to live up to an idealized version of yourself.
10. **Work towards becoming who you are:** When it comes to your shadow side, learn how to embrace it in a way that feels right for you. If you're more of a people-pleaser and find that your fears and anxieties are holding you back, you need to work on this part of yourself instead of just pushing it away. The more you work on your shadow side, the more honest and authentic you'll become. You will also feel less like a victim to your circumstances or other people's

behaviors and actions in life.

11. **Learn from your mistakes:** You may have learned from your mistakes by accepting that you're not perfect and there's a reason for the things that have happened in your life. However, if you don't learn from them, the same mistakes will likely repeat themselves. This is why it's important to learn from each situation to take appropriate action and move forward with positivity.

Chapter Six: The Shadow and Society

Let's begin with talking about the meaning of society. According to the dictionary, society is defined as a group of people who live in a particular place and share certain beliefs or customs. Society is a collective way of living that has arisen from our need to cooperate and coexist with other people to survive. But what about the shadow self?

Research by psychologists and philosophers such as Sigmund Freud suggested that the human psyche can be divided into three parts: a person's ego (or conscious mind), an individual's darker self (often called their "shadow" or "id") where repressed emotions are kept, and desires take form, and finally, the person's superego (their moral guide). So how does society interact with these split personalities? Well, it does so through culture.

Culture refers to people's everyday beliefs and behaviors in a society that are passed down through generations. As you can imagine, culture also influences these three personalities as it sets guidelines for acceptable behaviors and thoughts.

So how does this play out in our day-to-day lives? Well, for example, let's imagine a situation where one person makes a mistake that puts the whole group in danger, so they are asked to apologize for their behavior. After doing so, the individual will begin to reflect on their actions and believe that they did something wrong for which they should be forgiven. Although the person may feel slightly guilty about having made a mistake, it is not a feeling that will prevent them from making similar mistakes in the future. So, what just happened to this person?

The answer is quite simple; they became integrated with society. As mentioned before, the culture encourages people to behave a certain way and have specific thoughts, which in this situation means that everyone expects an apology after someone makes a mistake. In this particular example, it could be a new person to the group, a member who is out of line, or their boss. Whatever the case may be, they will use society's "standards" to guide them along in their behavior.

You may have already seen this in action right outside your home where you live, because it is quite common for people to apologize for speeding when you are sitting on your front porch. However, this does not tell you how these words actually affect their thinking process. We do not realize that when we make an apology to our neighbors and family members, these words are working on our ego by seeding guilt into our psyche.

But why should we be responsible for our actions in this regard? Well, that is one of the themes often touched on with the shadow self. Society will tell you to make amends when you have done something wrong, but the shadow self will not believe this because these transgressions are its own fault - and not yours.

This is one of the main problems with the shadow because if you continue making mistakes, society will grow tired of them and eventually reinforce the shadow's belief that they are worthless. So, what happens if we try to move closer with society but still have our rejected parts hidden away? The answer lies within us and can be found in finding a balance between our ego, individual self, and superego.

How the Shadow Self Is Rooted in Childhood

One of the most interesting aspects of the shadow self is how it is made up of very un-conscious traits that are not even thought about until later in life when they begin to surface. In other words, our shadow selves result from what was learned and modeled by our parents, guardians, peers, and other members of society that we interacted with during childhood.

Every trait exists because it was learned during our formative years when we were too young to realize what was happening. If this is not enough to convince you, let's go over a few examples.

Many children believe that they are not important members of society, which manifests in them feeling like they have no friends or family to turn to in times of need. Children who have lived with a single parent or had an absent parent figure will often struggle with feeling like they are not getting enough attention or love. Some children grow up to believe that they are not important enough to have anything special because their parents did not give them any of the things they wanted or needed.

While it is easy to see how these examples could turn into destructive thinking, it is also possible for them to strengthen the ego. However, it is the combination of how successful we were growing up and what kind of person we grew into that determines which personality traits became part of our psyche. So, let's go back to our example from before, where one individual makes a mistake and must apologize for putting the group in danger.

If this person was successful growing up and made a name for themselves in their chosen field, they will accept the mistake, learn from it, and move on. However, if this person had a rough time growing up, their response would be quite different because they would feel like they didn't deserve to move up in society. This will prevent them from seeing the situation as one of learning but instead seeing it as a sign of something being wrong with them.

Although some people have what is called an "invisible" or "shadow" personality, it can easily be seen when a person cannot differentiate between right and wrong. This is because the ego will usually turn to the superego to determine what acceptable behavior is. If it cannot determine this on its own, it will become confused, which will result in the person feeling like they have no idea what they are doing.

This is why there is such a wide range of behaviors with these personalities because some will violate societal rules and be what others consider immoral while they feel that their actions are justified. Therefore, individuals with these personalities don't have a moral compass that can cause them to make choices based on their impulses. This makes them appear irrational and unpredictable, but appearances can be deceiving because, most of the time, these choices are being made out of fear.

There are different ways to interpret what the shadow self is, but there is one thing that cannot be denied, it exists within us. The only thing that it needs to be successful is time to grow into a personality. However, most of us will never get to see our shadow selves because they are hidden beneath layers of denial, sorrow, and anger.

We will never integrate with them and become whole because these traits will remain isolated and unacceptable in a world where your actions determine your worth. This is why many people live their lives without ever getting to know themselves, and it is also a big reason why some of us struggle with depressive disorders.

This does not mean you should become defensive when you find out about your shadow self because it will only worsen matters. Instead, you need to be objective and look at your behavior from an outside perspective to see if any traits could be labeled as unacceptable. Remember, this process should never be used as a means of self-flagellation; instead, it should be used to better understand who we are as human beings.

How to Reintegrate with the Shadow Self and Society

When it comes to self-reintegration, you will first need to take a fair look at yourself and make sure that you are not avoiding the problem. For this process to work, you'll need to help your shadow self understand you accept it as part of the whole. However, for this to be effective, there are a few things you need to know about your shadow self.

The first thing is that it has a mind of its own and will act independently regardless of what we want or say. The second thing is that you'll only become complete when you accept all parts of yourself, including those you hate. Those who hate themselves will avoid anything that makes them feel negative, so they often carry on in life without knowing their true thoughts and feelings.

Therefore, they can't know what it means to be complete with every part of themselves because they have abandoned their shadow selves to shield themselves from experiencing pain. Now let's discuss a few ways you can help your shadow self become a part of your personal identity so you can find your place in society in healthier ways.

Recognize your hidden traits. Others hold the clues you seek: Most individuals with a shadow self do not know how many traits they have until the right situation arises. Therefore, when you recognize your hidden traits, it will be an enlightening experience for you. The next time you meet someone and have the rare chance to know more about them, pay attention to what they say about themselves and their thoughts. If you hear something that does not seem like it would fit with who you think they are, then there is a good chance that part of your shadow self is talking through them. Therefore, take the time to listen to what they say because it could be a clue as to what traits make up *your* shadow side.

Change your beliefs: If you want to discover more about yourself, a few things must occur before this. For starters, you will need to develop a clean slate mentality and start taking a hard look at your beliefs. In addition, you'll need to let go of any judgmental behaviors to become open to the things happening around you. When you do this, the next time society judges you for something and causes your shadow self to feel negative emotions; it will find an outlet for those emotions. Finally, when you learn how to accept and change your beliefs to match who you are as a person, there is no telling what kind of life we could lead.

Step into the person you want to be: While your shadow self will not really have a choice about accepting you, it is possible that you may need to prove yourself willing to accept it before it will hear you out and stop sabotaging you. Therefore, there are certain things that you can do to make sure that your shadow self knows that you are serious about becoming a part of yourself. For starters, you'll need to eliminate any fears and make sure that you have no reservations about going after what it wants for you. To do this, start working towards becoming who you want to be and stop thinking so much about how others might judge your actions.

No personality cannot be broken down into the three categories we have discussed above. When it comes to revealing our shadow selves, it is usually not a pleasant experience because most of us do not want to face the things which make us feel like we are "less than." However, when you learn how to look at yourself objectively, you'll find that you don't have to hide from yourself anymore to become whole again.

The Shadow and Self Sabotage

The shadow self should not be feared because it is a part of us that we all possess. The only thing we need to fear is the self-sabotage that happens when we neglect our shadow selves and refuse to acknowledge their existence. When this happens, the negative traits of our shadow selves will be isolated and eventually forgotten for good. This means that those who let the negative aspects of their personalities run amok will suffer from depression, anxiety, self-harm, and feelings of hopelessness, just to name a few. Though it might be difficult to face who we really are, it is far more painful to live a life where negative traits run wild.

Everyone will eventually come in contact with their shadow self, and the only way they will be able to know how to react to that contact is by knowing what makes up the shadow self. How does the shadow self sabotage you?

It will make you feel unworthy of what you want in life: This can lead to depression and, if left unchecked, will eventually lead to self-destructive behaviors. It causes you to have a low opinion of yourself, making you feel like nothing is ever good enough. The shadow self makes us believe that we are incapable of achieving what we desire out of life, which allows our negative traits to run wild without the proper guidance necessary to control them.

It will involve you in unhealthy relationships: When you are unaware of the negative traits which comprise your shadow self, you'll often find yourself in relationships with people who make you feel bad about yourself. When this occurs, the only place these negative feelings will go is into your shadow self, creating a vicious cycle of strengthening your shadow's stranglehold on your life.

It will make you sabotage your happiness: Sometimes, when we are unhappy with parts of ourselves, the shadow may decide that the only way to make ourselves feel better is by making others around us feel bad about themselves or by doing something to harm them. This can often be done by acting mean to the people we love and belittling them so that we can feel better about ourselves. This is a terrible way for the shadow to react because it does not create the best conditions for you to reach your full potential.

It will sabotage your relationship with others: Our shadow can lead us to become resentful towards others and make us feel angry at them. When you get angry, you often take actions that make the other person feel worse about themselves and make them question their worth. Sometimes, the wrongs your shadow perceives aren't even actual wrongs, and these innocent people may be completely unaware of having slighted you!

It can sabotage your finances: When you struggle to balance out your finances and try hard to secure your future, it is often because the shadow is trying to sabotage your life. This happens because when we are constantly reminded of our shortcomings, we often think out of fear that nobody would want us, and our talents and skills will be wasted or are not as great as we'd like to think. We feel hopeless about our employment prospects or spend money on unnecessary purchases, which only compounds our money problems.

The shadow self can also cause health problems: Ignoring your shadow can wreak havoc on your physical, mental, and spiritual health. It can manifest as a chronic health issue and can compound the matter by leading you to make decisions that only serve to exacerbate your health problems.

You could even assume you're doing the right things for your condition but not realize you're being lied to the precise choices that will keep the problem around for a long time.

It will cause you to believe that you don't deserve the things you have: When things are going well, your shadow self will find ways to convince you that you do not deserve the good things you're experiencing. It could turn out disastrous for you if you eventually listen to that voice. You may find yourself rejecting offers that would actually be good for you, for the most logical sounding reasons that beneath the surface are actually your shadow self grasping at any excuse to keep you from what you want.

For instance, you could have a life-changing meeting tomorrow and be all excited about it, but for some reason, you decide to have a tub of ice cream the night before, knowing fully well that you are lactose intolerant. But you think to yourself, "Oh, it's just this one time, and I'm celebrating! I deserve this!" Next thing you know, tomorrow rolls around, and your stomach is so messed up you can't even get out of bed. This is just one of the ways the shadow can sabotage you.

Shadow Work, Sabotage, and Society

From the previous section, you can see how with an unintegrated shadow, it can be hard to find your place in society when the shadow continues to thwart your best efforts at every turn. Whether you're about to cement your place in the world with a new job, a new project, or a new set of relationships that would be amazing for you, you might find it really challenging to do any of these things successfully if you haven't called your shadow by its name and chosen to address it.

It's possible to even seem "well-integrated" into society on the surface and still struggle with feelings of lack of self-worth. You could "belong" and yet feel like you don't really belong. There's nothing weird about that. It's your shadow convincing you of your lack of worth. So if you think you don't need to do shadow work because society accepts you, you'd be very wrong. The fact that society accepts you means that you've fitted yourself into its standards and buried certain aspects of yourself that society isn't okay with. However, you can't bury those parts of yourself, no matter how much you try. They will be still there, in the shadow.

Doing shadow work will help you find your place in society without feeling sell-out because you'll be able to have better boundaries around where you begin and end. As important as it is to be a part of it, you don't want to lose yourself in the process because if you do, rest assured your shadow will have lots to say about that, and you're not going to like it. Shadow work is vital so you can feel like you're an authentic person, true to the values you hold dear as an individual - while understanding your worth to society.

A Guide to Bringing Your Shadow to the Surface

Know that the shadow is always with you: Whether you're aware of it or not, your shadow is always with you and constantly has your back. You don't feel as though it's a part of you because the light is so intense that it blinds the shadow into hiding itself. It may seem like the light and dark are in complete opposition to each other, but they're not. They exist side by side in perfect harmony and balance. Remind yourself of this fact, and it will be more than enough to help you bring it to the forefront of your consciousness.

Keep a detailed journal, and reflect on your feelings at every day's end: The more you reflect on what you feel in the light when you wake up in the morning and how those feelings change throughout the day, the more you'll begin to understand where the shadow vibration comes from. When you know that your shadow is always there with you, making decisions for you in the background, regardless of whether it is feeding into what is happening or not, it will be easier to know it's time to bring it out into the light. It's not going to come out on its own.

Listen to the voice and embrace its purpose: The important thing when dealing with a negative self-image or feeling unworthy is not to reject the shadow's voice but instead listen to its intent and receive it emotionally. You can do this by asking it to show you things you are worthy of. You'll be surprised at the things that come up when you ask.

Ask for your light to surround and heal the shadow: As you learn how to work with your shadow and bring it into the light, you must call on your higher self and other spiritual teachers to help heal it back into full alignment with you. If you don't believe in anything, you could meditate. Your shadow will need love and compassion, which is what your light vibration brings. All shadows are worthy of healing, just as all emotions are worthy of love and compassion. Let this be a reminder that no matter what your shadow does or says, apply love to raise its vibration in alignment with yours.

Chapter Seven: Shadow Work Exercises

Shadow work is the exploration of your dark side, which isn't easy to spot. You can do shadow work on your own or with a therapist. Some people take the help of psychedelics as well, but that is beyond the scope of this book. Considering all you now know about the shadow, I bet you're more than glad to know that there's something you can do to become more aware of it, grow enough to stop letting it sabotage you, and also help you dig into the good that hides within it, like talents you may not be aware of.

Shadow work is a concept of having different aspects of ourselves and the banished parts with which we're trying to reconcile. When you choose to explore your shadow, you'll find many answers to questions that have plagued you for years about why you act the way you do and why, despite your best efforts, you've been unable to change or maintain change for long. As you do shadow work, you'll develop a stronger and deeper relationship with your authentic self and your soul, which means you'll become a fuller, grander, more ideal version of yourself.

What You Should Know About Shadow Work

You need to know that shadow work isn't something you jump right into and call it done within minutes. You're going to need to put in some time and effort, learning how to notice your emotions because you may have a habit of shrugging them off, which doesn't bode well for shadow work. You must pay attention to the way you react to things, and you've got to be intentional, which can take time. So, the more you do the work, the better you get at doing this.

If you're new to shadow work, it's a good idea to have a journal or a logbook to note the times and situations when you have intense reactions and emotions and write down the triggers for you. Can you think of times when your breathing got shallow, your head felt hot and heavy, or you felt like you just got sucker-punched in the gut? Those are the reactions you should start noticing. Maybe you also tend to get itchy and sweaty in certain situations. Note it all down, along with what's going on with you at the moment. You need to pay attention to these strong emotions because they're basically your shadow revealing itself. When you can note the emotions, you'll start to notice the patterns around them.

By doing Shadow work, you'll notice many layers within you. Pause for a moment and consider the times when you felt an emotion welling up in you to a point where you almost succumbed to it - and you tried so hard to figure out why you were reacting so strongly. You feel the way you do because an aspect of you has been dying to come out for a while, and it's no longer willing to be silenced. So, rather than shoving them back down, it's best to take a moment and think about what they could mean. Face your demons.

Notice that when we come across something, we have a tendency to make snap judgments and shut it all down. However, the more you judge yourself, the larger your shadow looms, and the more you rip yourself apart. Sit with your emotions instead. Before you get into shadow work, ask yourself:

1. Who are you?
2. What do you want?
3. What do you need to release to make your dreams real?
4. Who's the person you need to grow into to be worthy of those things?
5. How would you like to present yourself to the world?

We're about to get into the various shadow work exercises. Note that you can do them first thing in the morning or at night before sleeping. If you can't show up at these times, it's okay to do them whenever you have the time, but the important thing is to do them every day. You will need about fifteen minutes for each exercise.

Voice Dialogue

You may need: a journal and a sound recorder.

A journal will help you with the voice dialogue method.

https://www.pexels.com/photo/ball-point-pen-on-opened-notebook-606541/

With this exercise, you're acknowledging that your psyche is split into two basic aspects: the primary selves, and the rejected selves, the latter being the shadow and all things you've continued to treat as repulsive and undesirable. The primary aspects are the parts of you that you've developed to keep you safe in how you present yourself to others, which means that the creation and amplification of this aspect will lead to your unwanted parts.

Let's assume your primary self is someone who doesn't brag. That means your rejected self knows how to brag and enjoys it. So, here's how the voice dialogue exercise would work.

1. You're going to conduct interviews, asking questions of your primary self, the part of you that won't brag. To do this, you have to completely embody the person who never brags and describe how you see bragging. Ask questions like, what's it like to brag? What do you think of people you see bragging? Don't hold back in your answers. How long have you always considered bragging being undesirable? What's the earliest you recall thinking of braggarts this way? What do you think the consequences of bragging are? You can ask these and any other questions that come to mind.
2. As you ask these questions, please make sure you're validating this primary self. You want it to feel like you understand it and support it because it's a valid part of you that you created due to people not approving of you talking about your accomplishments. You could allocate anywhere from ten to thirty minutes for this part. Following these questions, the part you've suppressed will find it easier to come out and play. Then you'll be able to experience yourself as a braggart, and that will bring you to the conclusion that while you may have suppressed that part of you, it is still alive and well.
3. Interview this repressed self in the same way that you interviewed the primary self. Make sure to validate this aspect of yourself and allow it to brag. Acknowledge that it's part of you, and it's going to be much easier to be at peace with the act of bragging no matter where you encounter it. You can note down your answers in a journal or simply record them on your phone to review later if you wish.

Standing Up to Your "Good" Self

You will need: a journal to note your observations

If you're like most people, you probably think of yourself as a good person. Most of us do. The thing about shadow work is that for all the deliberate goodness we demonstrate, there's an opposite "badness" within us that balances it out, even though we've learned to repress it.

For instance, a person may consider themselves to be very meticulous and organized. It is a good thing and nothing to be ashamed of, but there's nothing wrong with not being put together either.

1. If you truly think of yourself as being organized, pause and ask yourself if you really are that way all the time.
2. Acknowledge that there are times when you're not as great at being organized, and you'll be able to make peace with it. The more you adamantly insist that you're organized and efficient, the more you repress and reject the part of you that isn't. That just feeds your shadow, giving it more power to come up and challenge you in the most unexpected and inconvenient ways possible. You have to be willing to embrace this part of yourself.
3. Make a list of all the things about yourself you consider to be true, and go through that list to acknowledge that there is a counterparty that exists to match everything you think of as who you really are.
4. Be at peace with the other aspects, and accept them without judgment.

Shadow Work Meditation

Meditation is a great way to learn about your emotions and their root causes. It can also help you learn to accept yourself more than you ever could without it. With meditation, all you need is yourself and a quiet place where you won't be bothered for ten to fifteen minutes.

1. Sit in a comfortable position you can maintain for the duration, and just pay attention to your breath.
2. If you notice that your attention has wandered away, you can simply come back to your breath without beating yourself up.
3. For each time you get distracted, accept that and bring your attention back to your breath.

Getting distracted multiple times in a session happens even to the best of meditators, so don't be mad at yourself for experiencing that. In fact, you should be thankful because the more you notice you're distracted, the better this practice will be for you because you're building awareness. This awareness will translate to noticing when your shadow rears its head and is about to sabotage you.

You'll create mental space between your words and actions and the impulses that cause them so that you can evaluate your choices before making them. Also, learning to do nothing but be in the here and now will teach you how to integrate the aspects of you that you don't accept right now.

You'll learn non-judgment and acceptance because you'll have thoughts flowing into your mind as you meditate. You just have to notice the thoughts but return to the breath. Don't judge the thoughts, don't criticize, or analyze them. Simply let them flow out the way they came in. You'll be able to notice your shadow self and, for once, try to accept it as it is, without judging. When you accept the shadow, it will no longer compulsively place roadblocks on the path to your success.

3-2-1

You may need: A journal and/or a sound recorder.

This is a method crafted by Ken Wilber, and you can either work with it as a meditation or use it in a journal. It is called the 3-2-1 method because there are three steps to do.

1. Face the issue.
2. Speak to the issue.
3. Embody it.

How does this work? You're going to take a look at something that isn't going well in your life, such as a problematic relationship with someone, and use that to gain some much-needed insight that will help you be more rational in your thoughts rather than overwhelmed by your emotional reactions.

1. **Face the issue:** Step one is to figure out who or what it is you're going to focus on in this exercise. It's usually better to do this with someone you're struggling to maintain a healthy connection with, but this doesn't always have to be the case. It's not an easy thing to be in the same space as someone you might not be able to stand, whether out of anger, spite, or lust. Or a feeling of being inferior. However, that will make this exercise worthwhile, so pick someone you react to strongly regarding emotions.

   Imagine the situation or a person in your mind's eye. Do your best to recreate what they look like. If it's a situation, do your best to replay it in your mind. When you accurately represent the person or situation, you should home in on the emotions they bring within you. You can either use your journal for this or speak your words aloud. Address them in the third person and talk about the things about them that you love or hate or are most drawn to or repulsed by. It's important that you don't think too much about what you want to say or journal. Just feel the way you feel and immediately put that feeling to words. You shouldn't censor yourself. Let it all out as it is; there's no one to judge you. Use third-person pronouns when you do this part of the exercise.

2. **Speak to the issue:** Now it's time to address the situation or person as if they're happening or standing right in front of you. Make use of the pronoun "you." You can journal or speak. For this portion of the exercise, you can ask the following questions, among anything else you want:

   - Do you know that this is the way you make me feel?
   - Why do you treat me this way?
   - What is it that you want the most from me?

- What is the lesson that you want me to finally learn?

With each question, pause, and listen. You're going to get an answer. You can say the answer aloud if you want or simply note them down in your little journal. If you're inspired to ask more questions, go ahead. Also, notice if the projection you've created has more to say other than the answers they've given you.

3. **Embody it:** Now, this isn't necessarily a comfortable thing to do, but it is an essential step. The traits and issues you've been avoiding are who you are, and it's time to fill those shoes. You need to become who you've been facing and speaking to. You're going to revisit the sentences you made in the first step to describe the problematic person or situation that your shadow has projected onto. This time, you're going to replace the third person pronouns with the pronouns "I" and "me." So, you might find yourself saying things like "I am annoying," "I am proud," or "I am scared." It isn't comfortable, again, but this is how you connect your conscious and unconscious aspects to finally feel balance and peace within you. You have to acknowledge that all of this is within you.

Now, to be clear, this is not meant to make you feel ashamed of yourself. You can accept that you're annoying or angry without feeling guilty about it or feeling like you have to hide your head. It's about accepting those truths about you while being compassionate. You should also extend the same feeling of compassion to the situation or person you addressed during the exercise.

Shadow Mirror Work Affirmations

You will need: a journal and a mirror.

You can also work with shadow work affirmations using a mirror. Unlike regular affirmations, shadow work affirmations won't always be happy and full of sunshine and rainbows. Some of them are meant to keep you grounded. The following are some of the affirmations you can use to help you deal with your shadow healthily. Make sure you're looking into your eyes with love and compassion using a mirror, and feel every word and what it means to you. Please note that you may fight them the first time you run through these. That's okay, but the statement's truth will hit you with time, and you'll be wiser for it. Here are the affirmations:

1. I will never get the parenting I'd have liked as a kid, and I'm at peace with that.
2. I can accept that while I'm special, I'm no more special than others.
3. I cannot claim responsibility for what happened in my childhood, but I'm grown up now and in charge of how I handle it now.
4. What they did to me caused me pain, but they did the best they knew to do at the time.
5. I have decided to always forgive because I have realized that's the path to peace.
6. I now accept that we're all able to build and destroy, love, and hate. And that's why we all deserve to be forgiven and shown mercy.
7. I can understand being bitter, but I now accept that it's not worth it and doesn't serve me.
8. I've made mistakes, but I'm not made of just mistakes. What matters is how I choose to make things right.
9. I'm at peace with the fact that I have made and will make mistakes. I also accept that I can always do better.
10. There are those who seek love through selfish and hurtful ways, and they need love the most.
11. I only need to be approved of and respected by one person, and that's me.
12. If I'm in a toxic situation or relationship, that's my choice. I'm free to walk away from it when I can find it in me to do so.
13. Any relationship or situation that makes me feel drained isn't worth my energy and time.
14. Other people's opinions of me aren't my concern.

15. While it feels good to have other people's approval, their approval means nothing in the end.
16. I am at home with all my imperfections
17. Having a terrible background doesn't excuse my terrible attitude. It drives me to be better.
18. I always see ways to improve, and I'm happy to learn every day.
19. I won't seek validation under the guise of looking for "feedback" or other input.
20. I alone am responsible for my happiness.

You can choose one affirmation to work with each day for fifteen minutes at a time, or you can work through all of these affirmations per session. It's your call.

Chapter Eight: The Ups and Downs of Shadow Work

You might be completely aware that you have things to work on but feel totally overwhelmed by the prospect of doing so. It's much easier to ignore it in the hopes that it goes away, but sometimes there will be a price to pay for not dealing with shadows in your life.

You might have noticed that when you take something away, something else gets added into the mix. When you learn to be more open and honest about your weaknesses, you'll get many opportunities to love and accept yourself as an imperfect human being. You'll learn how valuable you are as a person. There will be many ups and downs as you do shadow work, but it will be worth it.

Benefits of Shadow Work

You'll be forced to deal with the issue of your shadow self: As long as you're unwilling to learn about your shadows, you'll continue to have them. That makes you a victim of circumstance, and it doesn't mean that you have lost control as long as you know what is going on. Learning about your shadows will help free up some space in your mind where something new can become a glue that holds it all together. You go from being a victim of circumstances to an active participant in making things happen the way they should.

You're no longer living in the dark: You'll have clarity on where you stand concerning your life. You'll be able to discern your values and know what is important to you without being confused by your dark side. This will help you make better decisions about how you want to show up in life from now on, but you must open up and become vulnerable to what comes. The process of bringing your shadow into the light is not easy or always pleasant, but if you value your mental health, spiritual growth, and emotional well-being, then working with it will give you those things.

You will learn how to bring love and compassion into your life: If you've been beating yourself up for far too long, shadow work will help you learn to love yourself better. You'll stop being hard on yourself and begin to understand that what you thought was so wrong with you is actually not as bad as it seems. Choosing to do the work means you're going to realize you have no choice but to see your shadow side as worthy of love and acceptance, and this is a good thing for you because you'll also attract love from all around you.

You will have a better relationship with yourself: When you learn everything about yourself that makes you feel unworthy or unlovable, you'll develop the ability to embrace this new information and use it to improve yourself. As you begin to see your shadow as a good thing, it will begin to change in ways you never imagined. That's when you'll learn how to love yourself and the world around you.

You will be able to resolve feelings of anger and hostility: As you find out why you have so much anger in your life, it will help heal the source by providing a way for forgiveness and making amends for the wrongs that happened in the past. It doesn't mean that it will be easy, but it does mean that if you work through the process with an open mind, there will be healing along the way as things fall into place just as they should be.

You'll have an easier time making decisions: As you learn to see a larger picture of your life, you'll be able to make better decisions. You won't be running on blind faith because you'll have a far better idea of what is best for you and your life. It will become easier for you to trust yourself and follow through with your direction in life.

You'll manage to stay out of trouble: When you learn how to work with your shadow and start becoming a more spiritual person, you'll find yourself surrounded by people who are moving in the same direction as you. As you learn to love yourself after all these years of self-abuse, others will recognize that and become curious about what makes you different from them, but more than that, you will no longer be a magnet for trouble and drama.

Challenges of Doing Shadow Work

You must be willing to confront your inner darkness and bring it into the light: This is not going to be easy, and it may not be pleasant, but if you strongly believe in something greater than yourself and a willingness to explore your true potential, you'll eventually get what you need out of this process. Your faith in yourself will have to be strong enough for you to come out on top with less pain than you might experience otherwise.

Tip: Open up and let yourself be vulnerable with whatever comes. It does not mean you'll have to share what you know about yourself with everyone, but you might need someone who can provide a safe place for reflective self-examination. If you don't have a counselor or other professional that supports your needs, find someone who can give you the kind of support you need to get through this challenging process.

You will have to be willing to change your ways: Having healthy boundaries will help you in this regard. If you're willing to let go of negative patterns that have been haunting you for years, it will become easier to conquer them. You must be willing to grow beyond your comfort zone. It's easy to stay within your little world of self-controlling and self-pity, but once you get beyond that and allow yourself to embrace life with all its ups and downs, the process of embracing your shadow will become a lot easier on you. You'll have areas of comfort where the outside world has no place because that's how it should be if you want to be happy.

Many people struggle to change the way they've always behaved and the habits that have become ingrained in their way of being.

Tip: Keep in mind that this is the hardest part of a new life and accept it. Be willing to do some soul searching as you go along and embrace new ideas, perspectives, or ways of living.

You will need to look within yourself: The only way to see everything that is going on with your shadow is from within yourself. When you notice yourself acting a certain way or doing things out of character, it usually means there is something for you to learn about yourself. It could be a behavior you want to change or a way of thinking that you want to understand better. We all have a dark side, and depending on how we feel about ourselves, it can take us in different directions. It's okay to be afraid and get help if you need it. You don't have to do this alone.

Tip: If things about yourself are difficult to accept, it's time to face them head-on and deal with them somehow. There's no way out but through.

You must be willing to face the truth about yourself: People tend to run from the truth because they are uncomfortable with it. If you're willing to look at yourself through your eyes and learn as much as you can from the situation, you'll find things will become clearer and easier to handle. For this process to work, you must be willing to do what is necessary for yourself. If what is needed here is the truth about yourself, nobody else can make that happen except for you. You must be willing to confront your feelings without being too hard on yourself, and that may take a little time and patience. Some things can't be hidden from yourself any longer, and once they're out in the open, it becomes all too apparent what you need to do about them.

Tip: You don't have to love this part of yourself, but you do have to accept it for what it is and work with it somehow as you move forward with your life.

You need to be patient with yourself: In the beginning, you'll feel like this is the hardest thing to do, and you'll wonder why you took it on in the first place. However, as time goes on and you face one challenge after another, things will become easier for you. You're going to take one step at a time as you walk through this process, and if it's not entirely clear how it will unfold for you in the end, just keep putting one foot in front of the other until something happens that brings further clarity into your life.

Tip: Keep moving forward slowly but surely and do what feels right for yourself. With any new habit or way of life, it takes time for the past patterns to fall away, and in their place come new opportunities for growth and change. This is a long-term process, so give yourself time to evolve, grow, and become someone you want to be.

You will, at some point, have to forgive yourself: As it turns out, this is something many people struggle with as they try to change their lives because they're so hard on themselves and don't realize that forgiveness is what allows them to move forward and become new. When you forgive yourself, other things start to fall away as well. You have to be willing to let go of self-loathing and see yourself from a new perspective. As hard as it might be for you, let go of what has hurt you in the past to come out on the other side happy and unencumbered by your past mistakes.

Tip: Forgiveness is not always easy, but when it comes from within, a deep sense of peace settles over you. It's important for your good to learn to forgive yourself for any mistakes that have held you back in the past.

You must trust the process: Whatever process you're going through and however long it takes to get to where you want to be, it's important to trust it. It means having utmost belief and faith that whatever is going on with you will work itself out. It might not be entirely clear at first how any of this happened or what role certain people played in your life, but over time things will become clearer, and the changes will take place. It is not an easy task, and most people don't have the patience for it, so they give up when things don't happen fast enough. Take your time with this, and trust that life will bring into play what's right for you when the time is right.

Tip: If you don't trust yourself, it will be hard to take the journey toward your dark side. You have to trust yourself and your instincts enough to go with the flow as you try to make changes in your life. If you listen to others who try to stop you, you'll only delay progress since they won't know what is right for you any more than you do. Your higher self knows what is best for you, so let that part of yourself direct your journey into the unknown. Let go of fear and embrace what life brings with open arms and a willingness to learn from it no matter how painful or frightening it might be.

As David Schoen puts it in War of the Gods in Addiction, "The more cut off and unconscious we are of our personal shadows, the more vulnerable we are to having those shadows break out and be set free for a time by addictive behaviors." So regardless of your challenges, always remember that it's worth it in the end.

How to Navigate the Ups and Downs of Shadow Work

1. **Face your fears:** The biggest obstacle we all face as we try to navigate our shadow is the fear of what might happen if we allow ourselves to see where it really lives. We stand in denial and pretend there isn't any reason to be afraid because everything that has happened to us in the past is "just terrible." The reality is that the bulk of who we are has been formed from our experiences, and it's not going anywhere any time soon.
2. **Trust your instincts:** One thing that's not easy to do when you're trying to move into the shadow is to trust your instincts and forget everything you've been taught about being a good person. Actually, it's even harder than that because we have been told by our parents and society in general that there are certain things we can't do and may very well end up harming others if we don't follow the rules. We're taught to keep one foot in front of the other as we walk through life because all too often, life doesn't fall into place for us or meet all our expectations because of our "weaknesses." So, while we ignore our doubts, we deny the value of what is inside of us. We have no idea how important it is to explore who we are and accept the gifts that come with it, even though we might not

understand what they are or why they're revealed at this time.

3. **Stop trying at all costs:** If you want to move into your shadow and follow the path of change and growth, you must stop trying to be someone else and just be yourself. Once you accept that person is who you really are deep inside, it won't be long before you begin to see the world differently. You can't control what will happen because many things in life aren't meant to happen the way the plan is laid out. When you stop trying and just let things happen, new doors open up for you that have been closed for years.

Chapter Nine: Bringing the Shadow into the Light

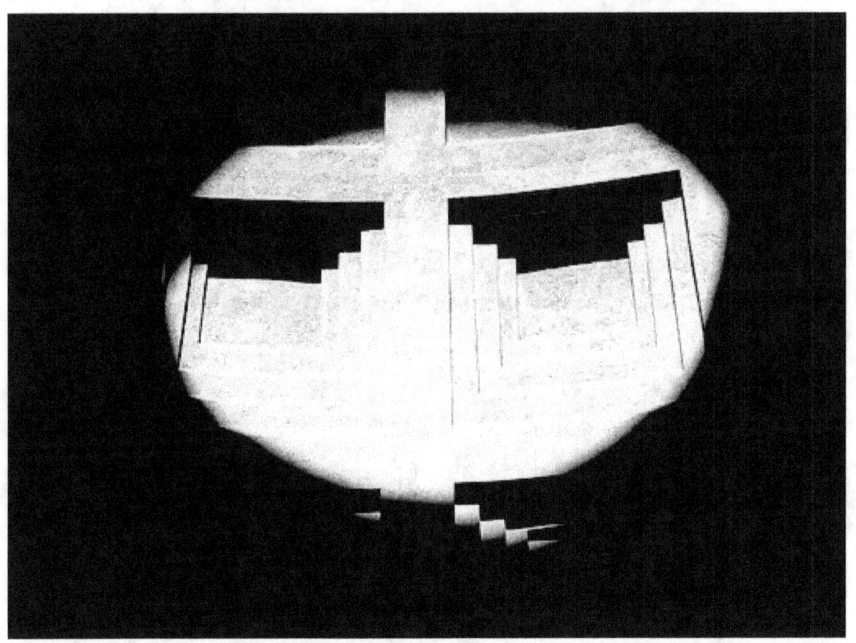

Bringing the shadow into light.

Wittylama, CC BY-SA 4.0 <https://creativecommons.org/licenses/by-sa/4.0>, via Wikimedia Commons: https://commons.wikimedia.org/wiki/File:Shadows_on.jpg

If the shadow is everything that we've repressed, then it stands to reason that the light is the part of us we've accepted. If the shadow sabotages us, then the light is our strength. If the shadow has taken over our lives, the light shines through to set us free. When we start the process of accepting our shadow, the next step is to bring it into the light where we can begin to live life on a new level. If you're willing to do this, you can get your life back and experience all that's possible for you in this lifetime.

Make no mistake as you see your shadow emerging in every aspect of your life. You'll be horrified by what is happening but, at the same time, thrilled to be alive. You'll realize that while you may not have all the answers, there is a power within you that has never been tapped before.

As this force emerges and changes your life in ways you could never dream were possible, you'll feel as if a part of you has been awakened from a long, deep sleep. You'll begin to see yourself in ways that go far beyond anything you've experienced before, as if there's so much more for you to learn about being happy and living life full-out. If this is the path for you, take your time and do things right, or it won't last. You have to be patient but also determined enough to see it through when times get tough because they will.

Draining vs. Energizing

This is a short and sweet exercise where you can figure out what your daily experiences are doing to your psyche. Here's what you need to do:

1. Get a pen and a piece of paper.
2. Create two columns.
3. Name column a "Draining" and column b "Energizing."
4. Consider the interactions that you go through daily.
5. Any interactions that drain you go to column a.
6. Put the stuff that energizes you in column b.
7. Figure out how you can begin to cut down on the stuff in the column.
8. You can do this for situations as well. It doesn't just have to be interactions.

Speak Aloud

Another way to bring your shadow to the light is to discuss it with someone you can trust and who has your best interests. They should be able to help you so you don't feel ashamed of yourself and do much better at accepting yourself as you are.

1. With what you've learned so far from this book, identify the shadow aspects you have.
2. Speak about these aspects with a trusted friend or a licensed therapist.
3. Talk about these aspects. For instance, you could find that you want to feel capable but were taught to only rely on others, even for the smallest things.
4. Go deep into the impact this belief has had on your life.
5. Talk about the different ways you could work with and integrate those aspects of your life.

Rainbow Bright Healing Tube

This is a powerful technique to show your dark side in your dreams. Everything you've ever suppressed will likely show up, so be sure you're ready for what's to come. When you have those dreams, pause to think that whatever you're afraid of isn't that bad. Here's what you need to do:

1. Sit in a comfy chair or lie on a mat or on your bed.
2. Close your eyes and breathe deliberately, allowing each inhale to flow into each exhale.
3. In your mind's eye, picture a rainbow. Make it the brightest one you've ever seen.
4. Visualize that rainbow encompassing your body like a tube. Notice how the colors glow even brighter than they were at the start.
5. Feel the colors of the rainbow go through you. Play with them like a kid.
6. Remain in this tube for five to ten minutes, or as long as possible, then go to bed or end the session.

Write a Letter

Every emotion is energy, whether you term it good or bad. No one on Earth is above getting carried away by the so-called *bad emotions* like worry, frustration, rage, anxiety, fear, etc. The trouble is, when most people experience these emotions, they would rather shove them down than go through them. Because we have been taught ever since we were little that certain emotions are simply not okay to demonstrate, even if justified. By now, you were well aware of the fact that that energy does not disappear; *it goes straight to the shadow.* The exercise of writing a love letter to your shadow is an excellent way to get in touch with it and bring some light and healing to it. Here's what you need to do.

1. **Pick a shadow aspect to deal with:** You have to decide which aspect you want to bring light to. Could it be your fear of being seen by others or your fear of scarcity? Perhaps you'd like to address the self-doubt that cripples you. Or you'd like to address the self-sabotage that has hindered you from attaining the heights you should. Whatever you like to address, make sure that you are specific. For instance, you can't just address the emotion of fear. Narrow it down. Fear of what, exactly.
2. **Get your paper:** At the very top, just as you'd start off an informal letter, say, "Dear [Name of Shadow Aspect]. Make sure to feel the emotion behind the word "dear" because you're trying to pull it close to you and shine love and light on it. So, beware of the temptation to be snarky in intent as you write that.
3. **Thank the Shadow Aspect:** The next line should begin with, "Thank you." Go ahead and thank this shadow aspect for everything that you understand. It's been created to keep you safe from or lead you towards. For instance, if you are dealing with the fear of death, you can thank this fear for keeping you protected from all sorts of harm and making sure that you stay alive. There is nothing to be afraid of when it comes to fear. It can be quite a positive emotion, but the trouble is most people don't think of it that way. When it comes to working with

your shadow, keep in mind that no energy or emotion is totally bad or good. The trouble with fear is not fear itself but the fact that we continue to ignore and suppress it and act like it is a shameful thing to feel it. If you pause to give this thought, you will find that fear has benefited you.

4. **Note down the ways this shadow aspect has been beneficial to you:** Now that you realize nothing is entirely good or evil, you can think of the different ways your shadow aspect has helped you and write them down. Make sure to come up with at least two different benefits it has offered you.
5. **Pay attention to the shifts within you as you write**: You may sense a shift in your thought process, energy levels, or emotions. Pay attention to your chest area and shoulders in particular. You may notice a reduction of tension and easier breathing, or it could be a warm sensation flooding your body. Note all the sensations you feel at the end of the letter, or if you prefer, on a different page. As you do this, it is important to recall that the letter is one of love because your shadow is not your enemy; it is simply an underappreciated friend that you're only beginning to realize has been of great service to you in the best ways it knew.

Challenges of Bringing Your Shadow into the Light

Consistency is not the easiest thing, but you must stick with the process: Just as the shadow emerges in stages, so will your experience of the light work. Whatever you may have experienced in the past, it's unlikely that you'll experience it again. At first, this feels like a letdown, but we have to maintain a certain level of commitment and trust that everything will unfold on its schedule. Remember, this process isn't an overnight thing. The one thing that helps me with this is recalling just how fortunate I am to know what I know about myself now compared to when I was younger. How have I made this much progress with my shadow? By staying consistent with the work.

Tip: Do not think of this as a one-time thing, but as a lifestyle of getting to know yourself. Consider yourself a lifelong explorer of your consciousness, and it won't feel so overwhelming.

You will be in pain: Learn to embrace the pain from the process. It's not a choice to be made lightly, though it is *precisely* why you need to take this journey. If you want to bring your shadow into the light, you'll have to give up many familiar things. You must stop looking outside yourself for answers to see who is inside. Your fears and doubts can seem overwhelming at first, but they will turn out to be beautiful gifts if we allow them to be part of our lives. You can't experience significant change without some pain, and bringing your shadow into the light is no different.

Tip: While you may want to run away from the pain and confusion, the fact remains that you'll be much better for having gone through all those emotions. Do not tempt yourself to remain where you are unless you're willing to continue to live a limited life. When it gets tough, remember that as you continue to bravely plant one foot in front of the other, it will be worth it.

You will feel vulnerable: Everyone experiences vulnerability as they begin to surrender to the process of self-acceptance. You can't keep your walls up and down at the same time. You'll have to let a few of them down even if they're hard to let go of. The more walls you're willing to take down, the easier it will be for you to bring your shadow into the light.

Tip: Remember just how vulnerable we all are as human beings, and that vulnerability makes us beautiful and brings us closer to others. We are entitled to those feelings because we all feel them at some point. Allowing this feeling is what brings us the greatest joy. You'll feel vulnerable in ways you've never felt before, but it's a price worth paying for your freedom and peace of mind.

You may have blocks you do not know how to move: It goes without saying when we begin to clear out the old and bring in the new, we can expect some resistance. The last thing you may want is a new way of being, even if it's better. I'm speaking about the issue of blocks along your journey. Because it's very difficult to walk your path, we all need help in certain areas of our lives, so opening up to other people who can support us will make a difference as we take on this challenge. No one person has all the answers, and there are no shortcuts when bringing your shadow into the light.

Tip: Each and every one of us has something that needs to be healed, so don't listen to the naysayers who tell you that this process won't work. Something deep inside of you is worth taking care of, even if it means making some changes to your life. The fact that there's a block also means that there's a breakthrough. Just be patient and take it easy on yourself. No one said this was a day's job.

The plan may not be clear enough for you: When we are speaking about how big the shadow can be, it can feel like we're talking about an alien life form we need to discover and understand for us to begin moving forward with our lives. I'm speaking about the issue we all have within ourselves, which can be so hard to grasp when we don't know where to begin. Sometimes it's hard to see the truth, especially considering how deeply it is buried in each of us.

Tip: Your understanding of who you are, and your life experiences may be limited; this doesn't mean you cannot grasp the concept, only that it may take some time. Keep moving forward on your journey and take it one step at a time. Like anything else worth doing with our lives, this takes practice until we get better. Be patient with yourself and keep taking those tiny steps forward.

You can't please everyone: The shadow will never be able to fully disappear until we no longer choose to be a victim, whining about not being enough for someone or something. We are all born with different gifts, and each one of us has a different opinion about the way we live our lives. You may not like certain people, places, or things, and they may not like you back either, but you'll still have to deal with them in this lifetime anyway. At the same time, you may find great satisfaction in knowing that you're here and making a difference in some people's lives by choosing to do this work to be a better version of yourself each day.

Tip: There's only one way to live our lives, and that's with a positive attitude. It's not so important what other people think of us because it's most important that we think of ourselves with love and acceptance.

Benefits of Bringing Your Shadow into the Light

You with will have more clarity: The better we get at seeing our shadows and truly accepting them for who they are, the clearer our lives will become. We all have a choice in this life, and it's up to us to choose whether or not we will learn from each moment as it passes by. We benefit greatly from the knowledge that prepares us for what's next in our lives when we do.

You will find healing: Nothing is impossible when you're ready to heal and allow yourself to be happy again on this planet. True healing can happen when there is a change before everything can progress forward into a better place. We cannot expect someone else to heal us, but we can lay the groundwork for ourselves through self-discovery.

You will naturally attract a better life: All of the people and experiences you need in your life will come to you when you're ready to receive them. Your intuition will guide you where to go and who to be with, so don't put yourself in a position where people and situations that don't suit you'll be able to control your thoughts or emotions.

You will realize that many of your blockages are emotional: The emotional self is difficult to deal with because the human body is filled with energy, which is what runs the show. If we can clear out some of the emotions that are blocking us from taking action and moving forward, then we'll be on our way to better beings who aren't afraid to be vulnerable.

You will feel more empowered as a person: When you're willing to take on this journey, you're permitting yourself to do something that few others can do: work through their emotions to find their true selves. This takes time and will involve an inner conflict, but it's all worth it when you get there.

You'll be able to love yourself: Self-love is the greatest gift we can give to ourselves, especially when we've come this far and done so much work. Love yourself and be proud of who you are and where you've been on your journey thus far. You are an amazing person who is worth every bit of love you may have kept hidden in your heart because it's time to see yourself in a new way that hasn't been possible until now.

You'll have a more positive view of life: The biggest task we can face is learning to accept that every moment brings us new things and opportunities. When we give ourselves permission to see this truth and step outside of our comfort zones, we can see how miraculous life is.

Quiz: Have I Brought My Shadow into the Light?

1. Have I been able to accept myself as I really am?
2. Do I have the courage and strength needed to completely heal my emotional issues?
3. Am I no longer afraid of making "too much progress?"
4. Am I willing to see the shadow in me as an opportunity to obtain clarity?
5. Will I be willing to go through the uncomfortable process of learning to love myself more?
6. Can I accept the idea that life is a miracle, and every hour brings something new?
7. Do I have faith that when I've done everything in my power, the universe will take care of the rest?
8. Am I willing to keep climbing when others nearby are losing their footing so that I can be on the path to success?
9. Am I willing to take this journey by myself and make changes that others can be a part of as well?
10. Am I willing to fight for what I want?
11. Do I have a positive attitude about the future and the path ahead of me?

12. Can I accept that each day brings something new and that each person, place, or thing has something valuable to teach me?
13. Am I confident enough in my abilities to believe that there's no obstacle too great for me?
14. Have people been able to tell me things about myself with no fear of backlash from me?
15. Am I willing to see the truth about who I am and the person that I'm becoming?

Chapter Ten: Shadow Work: A Stage of Spiritual Awakening

What Is Spiritual Awakening?

Spiritual awakening is a process where an individual gains profound insight into the true nature of the world and of self. In this process, one gains a sense of universal or cosmic consciousness, which can be described as a feeling of knowing everything and being connected with all things. Spiritual awakening is not simply a shift in thinking but also an intense emotional and physical experience that one may feel at various points in their life. Furthermore, every individual is unique in their own way, so experience varies from person to person.

How Is Shadow Work Essential to Spiritual Awakening?

When we are doing shadow work, we dig deep within ourselves and look at things we have kept hidden from the world by exposing them to light. It can be very difficult to deal with emotions that come to light when we do this. We may feel vulnerable or ashamed at some point during the process. However, that is the purpose of shadow work, and it can ultimately result in a spiritual awakening if you continue to push through self-doubt and shame.

Spiritual awakening is a process that takes time, effort, and commitment. You must keep working on yourself for it to last; otherwise, you may find your old ways creeping back in. Shadow work is a process in which one becomes aware of their weaknesses, negative traits, and imperfections to improve upon them. Shadow work allows one to take a more objective look at themselves and their place within the universe. This process can assist in realizing your true self, gaining personal empowerment, and developing identity.

Shadow work is essential to spiritual awakening because it assists one in watching out for the areas within themselves that are holding back progress in other areas of life. It also allows for a deeper understanding of oneself and personal growth. Ultimately spiritual awakening is about learning to see the entirety of who we are as human beings, and this includes all aspects of ourselves, including our shadow side.

How Shadow Work Exercises Can Cause Spiritual Awakening

Meditation is a shadow work exercise that can help cause spiritual awakening.
https://pixabay.com/images/id-5353620/

Shadow work exercises can cause spiritual awakening by assisting one in looking within themselves. Through this process, one can better understand their shadow self and ultimately learn to accept them for who they are. As we become more accepting of our weaknesses, our negative traits, and imperfections, we will understand that they are just part of the human experience and no longer a burden. Through practicing shadow work exercises, one will learn to love and accept themselves as they are and emerge into self-love.

Shadow work is essential to developing the ability to recognize ourselves within our surroundings. This process allows us to understand that we are not separate from each other or disconnected from the world around us in any way, shape, or form. We are all connected and part of one global consciousness.

Shadow work helps us become aware of our place in the world and cultivate acceptance for everything that is part of ourselves and our experiences on this Earth. This process allows one to hone their personal empowerment to live a life filled with purpose and fulfillment.

To achieve a true spiritual awakening, an individual must be willing to embark on a journey of self-discovery that may sometimes be uncomfortable. As previously stated, the initial phases of shadow work can be stressful and may make you feel vulnerable. However, if you push through these feelings, you'll begin to understand who you are as a person and your place within the universe. When this happens, it can have profound effects on one's self-esteem and sense of identity, which can lead to increased clarity in other areas of life.

It is also important to note that not all exercises will cause a spiritual awakening. Many spiritual awakening exercises, such as meditation and mindfulness practices, are designed to help one become more in tune with themselves. Furthermore, these exercises will leave an individual feeling calm and relaxed and potentially cause a spiritual awakening in the long run but will not necessarily prompt the process.

How Spiritual Awakening Is about Embracing All Aspects of the Self

As individuals become more accepting of the parts of themselves they were previously ashamed of or avoided, they will begin to appreciate and love these parts. Regarding the shadow, one must be willing to accept them for who they truly are to fully embrace them.

Our perspective of ourselves and the world around us is constantly changing. One's perspective on an aspect of themselves may change over time as well; for example, you may think you look fat at one point in your life but then lose weight later on and begin to view yourself as fit rather than fat or gain more weight and look at the past "fat" you as being rather fit. The way we perceive ourselves is not always an accurate reflection of who we are.

In fact, many individuals leave out parts of themselves that they have hidden from others or themselves to live up to societal standards or other expectations they feel they must meet. For example, some avoid their desire to help others and devote their time and energy to making money. Others might be timid or shy but try to mask it by being outgoing and aggressive. By avoiding one's "dark side," we are left feeling incomplete as a person and lacking a sense of self-love. This can be dangerous to one's mental health over time as well. As a result, it is important to accept yourself for who you are and allow others to do the same.

The shadow work process will assist one in facing the aspects of themselves they have been avoiding, to become aware of what they are, and to make peace with them. It will then allow individuals to release the shame or fear from these negative traits, emotions, or experiences to gain self-acceptance. This process can lead to spiritual awakening because once individuals accept themselves for who they are, their sense of identity will be enhanced, and self-esteem will improve.

Signs of Spiritual Awakening

You become aware that there's more to life than you previously realized: You may have thought that your life was pretty mundane in the past. Wake up, go to work, make money, and return home. Try not to step on people's toes, be nice to the neighbor, pay your bills, keep your head down and be a good citizen. However, as you begin to awaken spiritually, you'll discover that there's so much more to you and life than you ever thought possible. You will begin to wonder about your true purpose in the grander scheme of things and how you can make the most out of this life.

You become more aware of your surroundings: It's easy to get caught up in the hustle and bustle of everyday life and take things around you for granted. However, as you develop spiritually, you begin to notice more details about your environment, including other people, plants, animals, and how everything is connected. You'll feel a deeper sense of purpose and meaning in life as you reflect on how fortunate you are to be here at this very moment in time.

You feel a growing sense of empathy: Empathy is truly one of the greatest gifts one can possess for yourself and others around you. As you develop spiritually, you'll find that you're more in tune with the feelings of others and their suffering. You'll want to provide comfort and help ease their pain and suffering because it may remind you of something that happened in your life. Personal experience is a great teacher, so if you can relate to something, then maybe it's worth listening to.

You're no longer identified with your ego: One of the most important things that spiritual awakening teaches us is that we are not our egos. As we awaken spiritually, we begin to realize just how much our egos get in the way of living in the present moment. Not only is this an important lesson, but it's also a great one because when we are living in the present moment, we are also connected with our higher self. When you're not identified with your ego, you'll experience a profound sense of peace and joy because you're no longer living in the past or worrying about how you will get through tomorrow.

You discover the connection between all things: As your understanding of reality increases, your connection to the world around you and everything else in existence. You'll feel a deep sense of gratitude for being alive and for all that this means. Your heart will open up and begin to feel more compassion for all that is around you and for yourself.

You become more aware of your senses: As you awaken, you'll begin to be more in tune with all the different facets of your being and how they vibrate at various frequencies. You'll also become more conscious of how these frequencies can affect the emotions, thoughts, and behaviors of others. You will discover that it's important to allow yourself to be present at this moment as you're experiencing life.

You feel weightless: It's normal for people to feel insecure about their bodies because we tend to compare them with others' looks and build unattainable bodies for us. But as you awaken, you'll realize that you're far more than a physical body, and your thoughts, feelings, and behaviors are just as important as everything else about you.

You feel things more deeply: As we can accept ourselves for who we are, it's possible for us to feel everything that is happening in our lives at a deeper level. The deeper the emotion or feeling we have, the greater our ability to connect on a very personal level. We begin to search for meaning in our lives, and this quest leads us to what we believe is "true." Many have difficulty finding some sort of spirituality because they don't know where it can be found or if it's even real.

Stages of Spiritual Awakening

1. **Noticing spirit:** The first thing that happens is realizing that there is so much more to life than just the physical aspects. At this stage of spiritual awakening, you stop thinking about yourself and what you need to do to survive but start thinking about consciousness on a grand scale. You feel almost like a hero in a movie who has been summoned from their mundane everyday life to a grander adventure than anything they had ever

considered for themselves. There comes a time in everyone's life or the moment when things change you forever, and you realize that you cannot simply continue living the way you've always done. You realize the only options are to evolve or die. For some people, this pivotal moment could result from losing a loved one, a terrible breakup of a major relationship, a near-death experience, some grand illness, or losing a cushy job. It doesn't matter what triggers this moment for you, but it will happen if it hasn't already. This experience will trigger you to your core. It will cause you to realize that the way you've always looked at life is no longer appropriate for this aspect of your journey. It will shake you awake. When it does, you can either close your eyes and go back to bed or choose to go on the adventure that the event is summoning you to embark on. At this point, the smart thing to do is to heed the call because if you do not, life will create a new set of circumstances with the same old story to wake you up once more. It's not a pleasant cycle to get stuck in.

2. **Selecting your path:** At this point of your awakening, you come to realize that your worldview must expand, and for that to happen, you must choose a path to go on your adventure. This period is as exciting as it is scary and unfamiliar. Everything you've ever believed about yourself, the people in your life, and the world around you will be questioned, and you will be forced to change your stance on many things. This is the point where some people turn to religion, and others turn to spiritual practices like meditation. Others still would turn to psychedelics to explore their inner consciousness and the world's consciousness. Some will select multiple paths to find the answers they seek. No one should tell you whether or not the path you are on is right for you or not. Let your heart guide you.
3. **Walking the path**: You become a seeker in this phase of your awakening. You study everything you need to know about yourself and the world around you to connect with

the true reality of life. The further down the path you go, the more familiar it grows, but also new challenges will present themselves so that you are not completely comfortable. The typical expectation in this phase is that you'll go from using external frames of reference, like what you have and where you are in life, to your internal frames of reference, such as spiritual guidance and deep-seated intuition. When you have problems or challenges, instead of using the old ego-based formats of looking for external solutions, you're likely to just sit down and be still in meditation to find the answers from within. You know you're making progress along your path when you feel lighter and lighter each day, and joy is your regular state of being. You don't care too much about taking life so seriously, and you are no longer easily roped into the melodrama which is regular life for others. Another sign that you are doing well on your journey is when your desires finally come to pass with ease. Where you used to struggle long and hard to make your dreams come true, you now manifest them with ease and flow. Everything you are involved in is influenced by grace. You experience constant miracles and happy little "coincidences" in your life, taking you closer to your ultimate purpose.

4. **Losing your way:** This is another phase of the spiritual journey the sojourner must be aware of. No one said spiritual awakening would always be a bed of roses. On this path, you'll be forced to face your cognitive biases and the many ways you have continued to deceive yourself. You'll need to make peace that you were not perfect and have many shortcomings. The challenge set before you entails being willing to adapt, changing your thoughts and emotions and how you perceive things so that you are full of compassion and understanding. You might also find that certain things outside of you will come to challenge your newfound awakened self, and it is up to you not to give in to the temptation to quit on your journey. At this point, so many people sadly choose to go

back to the life they knew before they woke up. If this ever happens to you, don't worry. Rest assured that life will come knocking at your door again to wake you up once more. However, it's much better to keep going rather than start again from scratch. The things that challenge you may come in the form of your personal beliefs, limiting situations, actual physical enemies, or setbacks on your path. They keep you from getting to a higher ascended level of consciousness. All these are engineered to cause you to doubt yourself. But you must stay true to your path. As the great Robert Frost once said, "The only way out is through."

5. **Becoming one with your path:** This phase of spiritual awakening is transcendence. You realize how connected you are to all of life, and you no longer see the distinction between you and another. You can see God in everything. One may assume that to get to this phase, you need to accumulate a lot of knowledge and experience, but that's not the case at all. As a matter of fact, the way to get to this point is by letting go completely of everything that you think you know. You continue to peel back the layers of ego until there is nothing left other than pure consciousness or awareness, which is known as the state of I Am. No matter what stage of your journey you're on, even if you haven't awoken yet, this is the state that we are all seeking in the end.

Quiz: What Stage of Spiritual Awakening Am I On?

1. Have I recently experienced something that has caused me to question life?
2. Do I get the sense that there might be something more than my everyday routine?
3. Do I feel restlessness and dissatisfaction within me?
4. Am I feeling uncertain about the beliefs I hold about life?

5. Have I come to a point where I am desperate for change?

If you answered yes to at least three out of five of these questions, you are in the first stage of spiritual awakening.

1. Am I currently seeking a path to explore my spirituality?
2. Are there several paths that I have been seriously considering lately?
3. Do I feel a sense of fear mingled with excitement?
4. Is my intuition pointing me towards a specific teacher or spiritual practice?
5. Do I realize that once I begin this journey, I will not look back, and I am at peace with that?

If you answered yes to at least three out of five of these questions, you are on the second stage of your journey.

1. Have I chosen the paths and tools that I desire to use to explore my spiritual side?
2. Am I finding myself learning more and yet, desiring even more knowledge?
3. Am I starting to look within myself for answers instead of trying to control the outside?
4. Would I say that my life is a lot lighter now than before I started the spiritual path?
5. Have I noticed a lot more synchronicity around me?

If you answer yes to at least three out of five of these questions, you are under the third phase.

1. Am I beginning to lose my way on this spiritual path I've chosen?
2. Have I begun to notice just how imperfect I am?
3. Am I dealing with the discomfort of my cognitive biases?
4. Have I noticed a tendency not to be consistent with my practices?
5. Do I sometimes get so frustrated with myself that I want to go back to where I started?

Answering yes to three out of five questions means you are in the fourth phase, where you lose your way if you don't stick with it. Keep going. It's worth it in the end.

1. Have I found it increasingly difficult to judge anyone or anything because I understand they are part of me?
2. Has my thirst for knowledge been replaced by the satisfaction of simply experiencing life?
3. Do I now understand that the ego is not who I am but a tool to be used as needed?
4. Have I finally realized that I am greater than concepts such as success and failure?
5. Do I now understand that there is nothing to do but simply be?

If you answer yes, to at least three of these questions, you are in the final stage of spiritual awakening. Enjoy this, but also understand that awake people may fall asleep. If you ever do fall asleep, it's okay because how can you wake up if you're not asleep, to begin with? Awakening is an ongoing process. Don't ever beat yourself up, no matter what part of the process you find yourself in.

30-Day Guide to Spiritual Awakening through Shadow Work

Day 1: Sit down for fifteen minutes and simply pay attention to your breathing in meditation.

Day 2: Take out your journal and write down all the positive things about yourself that you can think of. Read through your list and contemplate each point for a minute or two when you're done.

Day 3: In your journal, write down all the negative traits you can think of. When you're done, go through the list, and do your best not to judge yourself. Just accept those truths without making a call on whether they're "right" or "wrong."

Day 4: Go back to the entry you made on day 2, and write the opposite of everything you noted as being good about you. When you're done, sit for about ten to fifteen minutes trying to recall times you acted "bad." Don't judge yourself.

Day 5: Do the mirror work exercise from this book.

Day 6: Pick a few affirmations from this book, about two to three, and focus on what they mean to you for just ten minutes. If you get any insights, you may write them in your journal.

Day 7: Think about a challenge you're facing, and then recall the first time in life you ever felt that certain emotion when you faced that issue. Journal about the challenge and the very first memory you have about that emotion.

Day 8: Pick one aspect of yourself that has kept holding you back and write a letter to it.

Day 9: Do the 3-2-1 technique for an aspect of your shadow that you want to address and integrate.

Day 10: Journal every insight you've had so far from your exercises from day one till this point. Note three ways in which you can do better in your day-to-day life.

Day 11: Spend time in a situation or with people that "trigger" you into feeling uncomfortable in some way. When you feel triggered, pay attention to the thoughts and emotions you have and journal them.

Day 12: Revisit everything you wrote down from the previous day, and think about how the attributes that make you uncomfortable about a situation or person are also within you. Think about ways in which you constantly, unconsciously have sought them out. Write down your discoveries.

Day 13: Sit down with your mirror and do five affirmations today. Pick the hardest ones for you to accept, and as you say each one, really mull over what it means to you.

Day 14: For fifteen minutes, sit and contemplate the fact that you aren't perfect. Look over the entry from day 11, and this time, get comfortable with the fact that people think and feel this way about you too.

Day 15: Sit in front of your mirror, and allow times that you've been terrible or done something you're not proud of to come to your mind. Allow each experience to play out fully in your mind's eye, and when you're done, affirm to yourself while looking in the eye, "It's okay. You did the best you knew to do back then."

Day 16: Do the voice dialogue shadow exercise as outlined in this book. Write down your insights.

Day 17: Do the "standing up to your "good' self" exercise as outlined in this book. Write down your insights.

Day 18: Speak with two to three close, trusted people. Let them tell you three to five good things and three to five bad things about yourself. As you listen, pay attention to any impulses you feel within you to disagree. Note down what they say about you. Note what you agree with and what you don't agree with. Sit down and ask yourself "why" on both counts. Write down your insights in your journal.

Day 19: Do the draining versus energizing exercise, and decide to do at least one thing to give yourself more energy and joy in life.

Day 20: Sit in silence, and reflect on everything you've learned from day 11 to this point. Note down any new insights that may come up within you.

Day 21: Do the "speak aloud exercise" in this book, and make sure you record anything you learn about yourself and how your mind works.

Day 22: Write another letter to another aspect of your shadow self you seek to integrate so that you can finally make progress in the aspect of your life that seems to be holding you back.

Day 23: Journal about one or two traumatic experiences from childhood. Find the thread to learn how it affects you right now as an adult. When you've got it, sit down in front of the mirror and repeatedly affirm, "Who I was back then doesn't affect who I am right now. I can choose to be better."

Day 24: Spend some time with those who make you feel good. Pay attention to what you love about them. Then, later on, write down your insights on their behavior. Sit with what you've written, and contemplate the fact that those qualities are within you, too. Notice anything you struggle to accept and follow the emotional thread to find out why. Write down your insights.

Day 25: Pick five affirmations from this book and use them in your mirror work today. Go as long as it is comfortable for you, and make sure you remember to feel the truth of each word; if you sense any blocks or trouble accepting something, journal about why.

Day 26: Do the voice dialogue exercise for another aspect of your shadow you would like to bring back home. Note down any insights you get.

Day 27: Sit in meditation today for just fifteen minutes, allowing yourself to feel nothing but love as you breathe. If you need help conjuring the emotion, think of someone dear to you or a moment in time when you felt nothing but love. As you end the meditation, visualize your shadow self in your mind's eye, and hug it tightly with all the love you feel within.

Day 28: Write a letter to the aspect of you that feels undeserving of love and good things. Contemplate and write about how this aspect of your shadow has tried to protect and help you. Thank it for its services and ask that it release you with love in your heart and true appreciation for why it had to do what it did.

Day 29: Do the rainbow-bright healing tube technique before going to bed. When you wake up in the morning, journal your dreams and see what insight you can gain from them. If you can't see anything just yet, come back to it another time.

Day 30: Contemplate everything you've learned from the start of this 30-day journey to this point, and write down anything that strikes you as profound. You may repeat this guide as needed for the next 30 days.

Here's another book by Mari Silva that you might like

Your Free Gift
(only available for a limited time)

Thanks for getting this book! If you want to learn more about various spirituality topics, then join Mari Silva's community and get a free guided meditation MP3 for awakening your third eye. This guided meditation mp3 is designed to open and strengthen ones third eye so you can experience a higher state of consciousness. Simply visit the link below the image to get started.

https://spiritualityspot.com/meditation

References

Casement, A. (2006). The shadow. The handbook of Jungian psychology: Theory, practice, and applications.

Chappell, S., Cooper, E., & Trippe, G. (2019). Shadow work for leadership development. Journal of Management Development.

Dourley, J. P. (1994). IN THE SHADOW OF THE MONOTHEISMS: JUNG'S. Jung and the monotheisms: Judaism, Christianity, and Islam.

Grosso, C. (2015). Everything Mind: What I've Learned About Hard Knocks, Spiritual Awakening, and the Mind-blowing Truth of it All. Sounds True.

Gilmore, J. (2019). Community Art as Shadow Work. Jung Journal.

Karpiak, I. E. (2003). The shadow: mining its dark treasury for teaching and adult development. Canadian Journal of University Continuing Education.

Kremer, J. W., & Rothberg, D. (1999). Facing the collective shadow. ReVision.

McLaughlin, R. G. (2014). Shadow work in support of the adult developmental journey. Lesley University.

Mayer, C. H. (2017). Shame–"A soul-feeding emotion": Archetypal work and the transformation of the shadow of shame in a group development process. In The Value of Shame. Springer, Cham.

Morley, C. (2021). Dreaming Through Darkness: Shine Light into the Shadow to Live the Life of Your Dreams. Hay House, Inc.